"What's the girl like, your sister?" my mother asked.

"Don't call her my sister," I almost shouted. "She isn't and she never will be. She's a weirdo. She's pretty, like her mother, but to get a smile out of her is worth your life. I think she hates me. She certainly hasn't gone out of her way to be friendly."

Trying to explain Fern was a pain.

Also by Hila Colman:

DIARY OF A FRANTIC KID SISTER

THAT'S THE WAY IT IS, AMIGO

CLAUDIA, WHERE ARE YOU?

SOMETIMES I DON'T LOVE MY MOTHER

ACCIDENT

THE FAMILY TRAP

WHAT'S THE MATTER WITH THE DOBSONS

DON'T TELL ME THAT YOU LOVE ME

MY FRIEND, MY LOVE

NOT FOR LOVE*

NOBODY TOLD ME WHAT I NEED TO KNOW*

JUST THE TWO OF US

A FRAGILE LOVE

HAPPILY EVER AFTER

SUDDENLY

*Published by Fawcett Books

WEEKEND SISTERS

by Hila Colman

FAWCETT JUNIPER • NEW YORK

A Fawcett Juniper Book
Published by Ballantine Books
Copyright © 1985 by Hila Colman

Library of Congress Catalog Card Number: 85-5665

ISBN 0-449-70206-5

This edition published by arrangement with William Morrow and Company, Inc.

Manufactured in the United States of America

First Ballantine Books Edition: November 1988

THIS IS JIMMY'S BOOK.
HE KNOWS WHY.

Chapter One

It was obvious that my mother had something on her mind. She's a neat lady who is creative and efficient—vague about housekeeping, cleaning and stuff, but sharp when it comes to things like finding a treasure at a tag sale, or putting a scarf on an old dress that makes it look terrific. But that day she made remarks that were pretty silly. "Looks like you're going to be eating nothing but oranges for a week, Mandy," she said, dumping a huge bag of oranges she'd bought on sale on the kitchen table. She pretended she was putting away the groceries but most of the time she was moving things from one place on the counter to another. And all the time she wasn't looking at me. That was the real test. When she talks without looking at me I know she has something to say that I won't like.

I've learned to wait. If I ask her what it is, she gets impatient and says, "Oh, nothing," and I may not hear it for at least another day. I like to get bad things over with quickly. The more she fidgeted the more I knew this was going to be something *really* bad.

"Did you have a good day in school?" she asked. My heart dropped. She was going to take her own good time to tell me whatever it was that she had to tell me.

"It was okay." Naturally I thought about my father. Had something happened to him? That's one of the awful things about having parents divorced and living in different towns. When I'm with one I worry about the other. Maybe I have a morbid mind, but when I'm with my father I think that maybe my mother got sick in the middle of the night and was alone, or forgot to stop the car at the STOP sign because she was daydreaming and got hit.

As for my father, I used to have terrible fantasies of his having a heart attack in the middle of the night when he was alone. But now that he's got a new job teaching at Lenox Hill School and is living on campus, my nightmare has changed to seeing him suddenly clutch his heart on the ball field (he's soccer coach, too) and slumping down in a heap on the ground. My mother says she hopes that someday I will put my imagination to better use than dwelling on senseless disasters and that if I was sincerely concerned about my parents I could keep my room neater. It seems to me that my room is the least of their problems.

I have been tempted to tell her that if I didn't have to live in two houses—with her during the week and with my father on weekends—it would be easier to keep one room neat. They don't know how terribly neat I'd keep it. But that's old stuff now. They've been divorced for two years, and I suppose that's the end of it, although I keep thinking there's a chance of their getting back together again. I can understand people falling in love, but what makes them fall out of love is beyond me. Even my mother says she and my father get along better now than they did before, and that must mean something.

But of all the disasters I had thought of, and I'd thought

of plenty, I'd never imagined the one my mother popped on me that evening.

It was dark by the time the groceries had been put away, my mother had made a bunch of telephone calls, and we had made our four-mile run up to the pond and back.

Finally, after taking her shower, she sat down in the living room with her diet soda and looked at me with a determined expression. "I have something I have to tell you," she said.

Now I knew it was going to be something even worse than I had expected. I felt all hot and peculiar, and I was suddenly terrified that maybe she had some kind of rare disease she'd picked up in the tropics last Christmas, or cancer or something. Although I'd been waiting for this all afternoon, now I didn't want to hear what she had to say.

"Your father is going to be married." She said it like someone pronouncing a death sentence, and she almost made me laugh. Not a happy laugh.

"Who's he going to marry?" I was in shock.

"He said you haven't met her because they met on his trip to Italy this summer. They spent time together and have been corresponding and talking on the phone since then. I think she just came back to this country a few weeks ago. Sounds like he was really swept off his feet." Her face was deadpan, yet there was irony in her voice that said, How could this happen!

"Is she Italian?"

"No, she's an American. I think she was on a tour in Italy. And, Amanda, I'm afraid there's more. She has a daughter a little older than you. Maybe a year or so. I'm not sure." My mother said it quite calmly, but the look she flashed at me was anything but that. She looked like someone watching a rocket go off and not knowing where it would land.

"A fifteen-year-old daughter? You can't mean it. He wouldn't do that." I honestly thought she was making it up.

"He will do that. Four weeks from Sunday. You and your sister are going to be bridesmaids."

"My *sister?*" I shrieked. "She can't be my sister, I don't even know her." The words were beginning to sink in. My father was going to be married, and he was marrying a woman who had a daughter almost my age. I sat down on a big pillow with my back to my mother and stared out the window.

It was late summer, almost fall. The maple tree outside the window had a few splashes of color, and that morning there had been a real chill in the air. I love fall, a time when my dad often takes me on long hikes. He knows a lot about the woods, and he spots tiny little plants I can't even see, and he knows all the long Latin names.

"Is she going to be there weekends when I stay with him?" I asked, hardly turning around.

"Of course. She'll be living with them."

Then I did turn around. "You mean she's going to be living with *my* father? Where's her own father? Why doesn't she live with him?"

"He's dead." My mother's voice was very gentle. She came over and stood behind me, her arms around my shoulders. "Your father says that she's a great girl and that you're going to get along fine. Once you said you thought having a sister might be fun. Now you'll have one."

"I never said that. I never wanted a sister. A brother might not be so bad, but a sister. . . ." I turned around, and before I knew it I was sobbing into my mother's lap. "He shouldn't do that," I sobbed. "It's not fair. He's *my* father, no one else's . . . I hate her. I don't want to know her . . . I hate her mother, too, and I'm not going to be anything at her stupid wedding. . . ."

4

My mother held me close and ran her hand over my hair. "Don't carry on so," she said in her soothing voice. "You haven't met her yet—don't decide that you don't like her. Give yourself a break, and the girl, too. Her name is Fern, Fern Hopkins. But I guess when her mother gets married she'll become Fern Maynard—your father thought it would be easier if both his daughters had the same name."

I sat upright. "Fern—that's a ridiculous name. Fern Maynard. That's awful. She is not Dad's daughter and she has no business being called Maynard."

"It's your father's idea, not hers."

"Why hasn't he told me all this? Why you?"

My mother smiled. She has a strong face, serious and determined, like pictures of peasant women standing in their fields looking as if they will be there forever. But when she smiles her face gets soft and looks as if someone put a light inside her. "I think he was scared. He was afraid you'd get upset. Your father doesn't like to face anything unpleasant. He'd rather let me do it." She laughed. "You know how he is. Remember the time his suit came back from the cleaners ruined? He wouldn't take it back; I had to. He would have thrown the suit away rather than face the cleaner. I think he thought that if I accepted his getting married again, you would, too."

"Do you like the idea?"

"I don't like it or dislike it. He has every right to get married. I only hope it's not going to be difficult for you or change things between us. But you're the one I care about." My mother is very controlled, but I could see that she wasn't any more thrilled by this marriage than I was. So far my parents didn't fight the way other divorced parents I knew of did, but obviously a new wife could upset everything. "I think it's time we had some supper," she said determinedly. "I'm getting hungry."

5

"I am, too." It takes a lot to kill my appetite, but when we sat down in the kitchen to eat, I wasn't all that interested in food. Fern Maynard. The more I said the name, the more I hated it. Amanda is my name, and Amanda Maynard sounded right. David Maynard, my father, Hester Maynard, my mother—all our names sounded right.

"What's her name?" I asked my mom. "The woman Dad is going to marry?"

"Ellen. Ellen Hopkins, but she'll be Ellen Maynard soon."

"Then there'll be two Mrs. Maynards. Won't that be peculiar."

"Dad's mother is Mrs. Maynard, too. And your Aunt Anna. There are lots of Mrs. Maynards. One more won't matter."

"One too many," I said glumly.

"At least when you get married you won't be Mrs. Maynard," my mother said brightly.

"I probably won't be Mrs. anybody. Besides, I can still be Maynard if I want to be. When Ms. Simon, my social studies teacher, got married, she didn't change her name. She's still Ms. Simon. Daddy's friend could keep her own name."

"I guess she doesn't want to. Let's not talk about her anymore. I want you to enjoy your dinner."

I didn't say anything, but the knot at the pit of my stomach told me I was unlikely to enjoy anything ever again.

The next morning when I got to school, after walking six blocks in a drizzle, a terrible thought struck me: If that girl was going to live with my father, she'd be going to Lenox Hill School. That really shook me up. Before my parents got divorced I went to a good private school where my father had been teaching. But when they split, Dad quit his job and took a year off, and Mom wanted me to go to a public school. She said it would be good for me. Actually, I think it was because she didn't want to spend the money, and she didn't want my father paying for it, either. She's terribly independent and makes a big thing out of taking only a minimum amount from him for me. Frankly, I think she has a cuckoo idea that if I get a lot of stuff from him I'll love him more than I do her, which is crazy. I'd love them both if they never gave me a thing. That is, I hoped I'd go on loving them both. The idea of sharing my dad with a new wife and another daughter was killing, and I wondered if I would still be able to love him the same. It was like some kind of betrayal. My parents getting divorced was bad enough, and I was just becoming used to that, not dreaming so much of a reconciliation anymore. And now this. A kid can take just so many jolts. My whole life had been changed once, and it had taken me most of the past two years to get used to all the adjustments of the divorce. I didn't think I could take another shock—especially one as big as a new stepmother and sister!

And knowing that that girl would be going to a school that is supposed to be one of the best in New England while I was going to crummy Region 16 Junior High didn't make matters better. They were cutting the budget so much all the time that the really interesting courses like modern literature and political science were being dropped. It wasn't fair.

I wasn't sure I wanted to talk about it, but my friend Mary Hayes took one look at my face and said, "What's the matter with you?" She looked so concerned I put my arms around her.

"Don't worry, I'm not coming down with some awful disease. At least I don't think so. But I got some bad news last night."

7

After that, naturally I had to tell her. I hate it when someone gives me a hint of something and then won't tell the rest. "Maybe she'll be someone you like," Mary said, trying to be helpful. "It might be fun. What will she be to you, a stepsister?"

"She'll be a pain in the neck, that's what. I hate the whole idea of a stranger living with my father."

"You're jealous."

"I sure am. Wouldn't you be? She's going to be right there in the same house, seeing him all the time. I only see him on weekends, and not every one at that. I bet now he'll see me even less." I almost burst into tears.

"I'm sorry," Mary said, and put her arm around my shoulder. "I hope she's cross-eyed and has fat legs."

As Mary often does, she made me laugh when I was depressed. She is the best friend I ever had. Outside of my parents I love her more than anyone. Sometimes I only have to look at her and laugh. She has that kind of a face, full of humor, with her snub nose, a few freckles, and terribly bright brown eyes. But even laughing Mary couldn't help me get rid of the heavy feeling I carried around the whole day.

Chapter Two

That Friday was the day. As usual, I was to take the hour bus trip after school to my father's house for the weekend. But that Friday was not usual. *They* were going to be there: my future stepmother and her daughter, Fern. My father had called me Thursday night and told me that he was very excited about my meeting them. He was also glad, he said, that my mother had told him I took the news so well. He had been worried that I might be upset. "You're a great kid," he said. "I'm proud of you." He made me feel like a louse.

"You lied to him," I said to my mother after I'd hung up the phone. "I'm not taking his big news well, and I'm not a great kid. I'm miserable and I'm jealous."

"You have nothing to be jealous of. Your father loves you—you know that. He'll never love anyone else the same way. Now, stop sulking and come over here. I need your opinion. What do you think of this pattern for plates? Don't you think they'd be pretty in a country house?"

My mother is a housewares designer whose job is to think up new gadgets and patterns. She was at her drawing board, painting a lot of different-colored flowers. She had her cassette recorder going with a tape from an old Benny Goodman record and was munching from a bowl of pretzels. She always seems as if she's having a good time when she's working, and it looks so easy it beats me why she gets paid so much money for her designs. She says she doesn't get paid half enough.

"I'm not sulking; this is serious. Your only daughter is feeling terrible and you ask me about plate designs. I suppose next you'll go off and get married, too. Are you still seeing that guy who took you to the disco? The one with the beard?"

My mother gave me one of her looks. A warning signal. "He has a name. Craig English. I may see him again. But don't worry about my getting married—I have no intention of getting involved."

"That's what you say. What should I wear tomorrow?" The nervous feeling I'd had all week was coming to a head like a boil.

"Come on, we'll look at what you've got." My mom got up and we went into my room. She's like that: One minute all absorbed in her work, but when I need her, she knows and she drops everything. She's terrific.

After we went through my entire wardrobe, I decided I'd wear what I always wore. I wasn't going to get dressed up for Fern or her mother. So I had on jeans, a jersey top, and a sweatshirt when I got off the bus on Friday afternoon. I had an armful of schoolbooks, and as usual, I trudged up the hill wearily from the village to the green where the school was. It was a pretty school with very New England-looking white clapboard buildings, tall trees, and huge lawns: The old part of the school—schoolrooms and some dorms—was on one side of the road, and the newer buildings—an auditorium and gym, and the tennis courts and ball fields—on the other.

Farther up the hill there was a hockey pond, some faculty cottages, and the Ivy House, a remodeled old mansion where the headmaster lived.

My father had a cottage set off by itself behind a row of hemlocks, with two huge oak trees in front of the house. Since Dad's a great gardener, the minute he moved in during the summer he planted flowers all over the place, and now in the fall, the marigolds and mums were still blooming. All of a sudden I got mad. Why was he living in such a pretty place when my mom and I were in a dinky apartment on a not-so-great street? Deliberately I blocked out of my mind that Mom had picked the neighborhood because it was interracial, that she—and I—liked living where there were movies, people, and sidewalks, and that my father's house wasn't his, but the school's.

I thought seriously about turning around and going home. I didn't have to stay if I didn't want to—I didn't have to meet his future wife and his new daughter, and I didn't have to spend the weekend with them. I sat down on a stone wall alongside the road and dropped my books on the ground, hugging the thought that no one could stop me from leaving. No one could make me stay if I didn't want to. I guess that knowledge alone, that I could leave anytime, sold me on staying. Besides, I was curious. What were they like?

I found the key where my father always left it if I got there when he was out. I took it from under a loose stone on the small terrace in front of the door, and I went inside. The house was quiet and I knew no one was home.

But immediately I saw signs of a new presence. Ellen What's-her-name must have been up here sometime during the week. The furniture had been rearranged and there were three hanging plants that had not been there before. The plants were a surprise because, while my father was a

11

gardener, he had an aversion to houseplants and had never let my mother keep any. That and the neatly stacked pile of journals and newspapers made me wonder what my mother would say. My mom's not the neatest person in the world, but the way my father used to leave his voluminous piles of papers and magazines all over the living room could spark off a fight. Sometimes, to keep the peace, I would sneak in before she saw them and pile them up. Was he doing it now or was this the work of his about-to-be wife?

Things were different all over the house. In the kitchen there was a brand-new dishwasher, also a note my father had left, saying that he'd gone to the airport in Boston to pick up Ellen and Fern. They were flying up from New York. New York explained a lot; they were going to be fashionable and snobby. That gave me a bright thought: They would probably hate living in small Lenox Hill since it had nothing in it but the school. The nearest movie was at least five miles away.

When I opened the fridge to get out some peanut butter, I couldn't believe what I saw. Usually it was pretty empty since my dad took me out to dinner on Friday night, and on Saturday morning we shopped together to get what we wanted, most likely spaghetti, salad, and ice cream. Today the thing was loaded: a big roast beef, cold cuts, cheese, fruit juices, eggs, bacon, and lots of stuff for salad. Seeing all that food made me totally depressed. Thinking of my father going out to buy all that for them—without me— made me feel really shut out. On the kitchen table I saw his list: Friday night, chicken; Saturday lunch, cold cuts; Saturday night, roast beef; Sunday, bacon and eggs; Sunday night, leftovers or go out.

He never did all that for me—not that I would have wanted it. That darn full refrigerator hit me more than anything with how different everything was going to be. My dad and I didn't need to fuss with all that stuff. We could have a wonderful time just opening a can of ravioli. I sat at the kitchen table and cried until I felt sick.

When I heard the car in the driveway I ran into the bathroom, quickly doused my face with cold water, and was ready to open the door for them. My father was lugging two huge suitcases up the walk, and Ellen and her daughter were still taking boxes and small luggage out of the trunk of the car. I suddenly realized they must be moving in, right now!

When Ellen saw me she put down everything and came running up the walk. The next thing I knew her arms were around me in a tight hug and she was kissing me. "Darling Amanda, you're exactly as I pictured you from the photographs your father showed me."

She stood back and held me at arm's length. "I knew you'd be pretty—how could you not be with David as a father—but you're even prettier than I expected. How wonderful to have two beautiful daughters. Come here, Fern, and meet Amanda."

Secretly I had hoped that when I met them some magic would take place and all my unpleasant feelings would drop away—that because I loved my father and he loved them, everything would fall into place. But I stood there, outside my father's house, feeling totally out of place, as if I didn't belong. Mostly I was embarrassed. Mrs. Hopkins had to be putting on an act. She couldn't be that gushy and bubbly about meeting me. She had her arms around me and her daughter and was laughing and babbling about how wonderful it was to have two daughters. How could my father stand it?

I had to admit that Ellen was a very pretty woman. She looked older than my mother and was entirely different. Ellen was full of gestures, while my mom was pretty calm. Mom had a healthy tan glow and never used makeup. Mrs.

Hopkins was delicate looking, with a narrow, aristocratic nose and dark blue eyes, deepened by lots of eye shadow, eyeliner, and mascara.

Fern and I looked each other over, and I was sure she was as uncomfortable as I was. She wasn't as pretty as her mother. She was taller, with the same remarkable eyes, but her features were stronger, and there was nothing fragile about her. Where her mother seemed small and cuddly, Fern, in spite of her curves, was cool and terribly sophisticated. Lots of makeup, textured black stockings, and shoes with little curved heels. Although she was only a little older than me, she looked at least eighteen. She was the kind of girl I had always steered clear of, the kind who made me feel awkward and babyish, conscious of still being pretty flat, with long legs and hair that kept falling over my face.

With Ellen Hopkins's arms around each of us, the three of us walked toward the house. Fern and I barely said a word to each other, and I felt it was just as well that her mother kept on talking. "This is Fern's first visit here. I know she's going to just love this house. She's frightfully excited about living at school—all those marvelous-looking boys around. I would have swooned when I was a girl if I'd had such an opportunity. I had to go to a prissy girls' school, and when the boys came to a dance we were surrounded by chaperones. I remember one time . . ."

"Mother," Fern interrupted her, "I don't think Amanda is interested in what happened to you at a dance over twenty years ago."

"Well, she might be," her mother replied mildly.

By this time my father had deposited the suitcases inside the house and came outside. At last he greeted me with a kiss, but it was already obvious that I was not to get that undivided attention I was used to when I arrived. I could see he was nervous. He didn't ask me about school, or say how pretty I looked, as he always did, but startled me by saying instead, "Don't you have any skirts? Do you only own jeans?" He had never said such a thing before, but I followed his eyes to Fern's pleated plaid skirt.

"I always wear jeans when I come here," I said firmly. "They're comfortable." He was fussing with the luggage Ellen had left on the ground when she came to greet me, so I'm not even sure that he heard.

I had been wondering all this time where everyone was going to sleep, since my father's house isn't very big. I had a neat room, complete with a big four-poster with a ruffled skirt and a cozy patchwork comforter, and my father had his own bedroom. He had also made a third room upstairs into a study that doubled as a guest room with a convertible sofa. There was a small junk room that had everything in it from a box of my father's baby blocks to his old college typewriter.

"I can bring some of this stuff upstairs if you tell me where to put it," I said to my father when we were all in the downstairs hall. I was dying to satisfy my curiosity.

My father hesitated before answering. "Ellen's going to use the study for the time being, and I thought Fern could go in with you. We'll get another bed, but in the meantime we can put up a cot."

No way was I going to share a room with that character. "Put the cot in the junk room. I'll use that."

My father put down the suitcase he was holding. It was the first time he really looked at me. "There's no need for you to give up your room, Amanda. This is only temporary anyway. After the wedding we plan to break down the wall and turn the study and junk room into a nice room for Fern. The school's given me the okay to do it."

"In the meantime I'll sleep in the junk room," I said. "I want to."

15

My father gave me a warning look. Ellen spoke up in her sweet, rather high voice. "Fern can sleep there. I wouldn't dream of putting Amanda out of her room. I know how young girls feel about their own room, darling."

"I couldn't care less where I sleep," Fern said, making me feel like a jerk.

So while Ellen was putting her things away, and Fern went outside to look the school over, and my father was preparing dinner, I spent the next hour or two dragging the stuff out of the junk room and up into the attic. When the room was cleaned out I put up the cot, took a chair from my room, and asked my dad where Fern was going to put her clothes.

"We'll pick up a chest of drawers tomorrow. Ellen figured out a place for more closets when we make the two rooms into one. It's all going to work out fine. Amanda," he put his hands on my shoulders, "I'm counting on you to make Fern feel at home. This is a big change for her, you know. She's been living in New York for the past few years."

She could have stayed there, I thought to myself. "I'll only see her some weekends."

"What do you mean *some* weekends? Nothing's changed about that."

"I don't know. I may have basketball practice on Saturdays."

"You're making that up. Amanda," my father said sharply, "don't make this difficult. Give me a break. I love Ellen and I hope you will get to love her, too. She and Fern can add to your life. You will have a real family here."

"I have a real family with Mom. She's a real family."

"Yes, of course. I'm not putting your mother down, but you don't have much of a homelife, with Hester working and you being alone so much. Ellen wants to make a real

16

home for you and Fern—for me, too. She's a wonderful woman; you'll see for yourself."

"I'll tell Fern not to unpack her clothes until tomorrow when she'll have a bureau," I said abruptly, and went upstairs to my room and closed the door.

My room was at the back of the house, and from my window I could see the ball fields, the tennis courts, and the hills beyond. Some boys were kicking a football around, and two of the four courts were being used. Mixed doubles on one court and two girls in white shorts on the other. They all looked as if they were having a good time. The scene was both peaceful and active, as if the kids were not disturbing the quiet of the countryside, but belonged there.

I was the one in turmoil. I had finally adjusted to living in Canfield, an old mill town that was slowly coming to life with a few new factories (including the china factory, one of my mother's clients). I'd made new friends and gotten used to the public school there. But now I was furious again and wildly jealous of Fern, who was going to be living at Lenox Hill with all the fantastic advantages it had. But of course it wasn't just Lenox Hill. My father was going to be her full-time father, and knowing him as I did, I could see him bending over backward to make her feel welcome and loved. I would never be first with him again. We wouldn't have our silly private jokes—what my father calls our prattle—our bike rides, our wild games of Scrabble. She would always be there.

The more I thought about it, the worse I felt. This was not like anything else that had ever happened to me because it would never go away. When I had the mumps, I knew they would eventually disappear. When I broke my arm falling off my bike, I knew it would get well again. When I felt sick worrying about an exam, I knew once it was over I'd be okay. But Fern was going to be my father's daughter for the rest of her life, and the rest of my life. The thought was unbearable.

Dinner that night was weird. My father was beaming and acted like the big, genial host, while Ellen kept chatting away like a character in a TV sitcom. She just loved everything: The chicken was divine—where had my father gotten fresh tarragon?—the rice was perfect, not mushy, and on and on. I had never known my father was so into food and took so much pride in cooking. He never used to pay that much attention to what he ate, and when he was with my mom he never went into the kitchen to help make dinner. Maybe he'd changed since he'd been living alone, or maybe Ellen brought that out in him.

I was glad, I suppose, to see him happy, but I couldn't help thinking, If only Mom had played up to him more, the way Ellen did. A useless thought. My mother never could act that way, not in a million years.

Neither Fern nor I spoke more than a few words. When the meal was over, Ellen insisted that she and my dad would clean up. "You two girls need some time to get acquainted," she said brightly.

The kiss of death. Like telling someone to be funny. "Would you like to hear some of my records?" I asked Fern.

"Okay, if you want." She was less than enthusiastic, but she followed me up to my room.

I put on my newest album, and we both sat glumly listening. "Do you come here every weekend?" She finally broke the silence.

"I have been. Why?"

"I don't know. It must be a drag, going back and forth all the time."

"I don't mind." I wasn't going to unload anything on her. "I always have a good time with my dad."

She looked disappointed at that statement. Then she gave me a funny smile. "You hate us, don't you?"

I'm sure that weirdo would have liked me to say yes. But in seconds her face closed up again, revealing nothing. "I've got to get used to it," I said lamely. "Don't you have to?"

She shrugged. "I guessed over the summer, when my mother wrote me about your father. She's nuts about him." From her tone of voice, I had the feeling she didn't think much of her mother's choice, and that irritated me. She and her mother both were darn lucky to get my father. It was all right for me to resent them, I thought to myself only half-jokingly, but, boy, they'd better appreciate what they were getting. The house, the school, a terrific man. . . .

Lucky for her she didn't pursue the conversation, or say anything about my dad. I'd have let her have it. But I was already beginning to learn that Fern was pretty close-mouthed about her feelings. She had that look on her face that said, I'm keeping my thoughts to myself. I'm not telling you anything.

I played one more record and then she said she was tired and was going to bed. I wasn't sorry to see her go.

After she left I got undressed and into bed, and wondered if my father was going to come up to say good-night to me. If he did, I didn't know it. I was so exhausted from so many emotions I fell asleep soon after my head touched the pillow.

Chapter Three

I hate waking up in an empty house. It was creepy to think that everyone had gotten up and I hadn't heard a thing. Besides, it was mean of my father not to have woken me up. I knew he'd say I must have needed the sleep, but he wasn't doing me a favor by leaving me in bed and going off with Fern and Ellen.

When I went downstairs I found a note in the kitchen saying he'd had soccer practice and they'd gone along to watch. He wanted me to come and join them. I didn't mind eating my breakfast alone; I was used to that since my mom was usually up before I was or slept later. But I felt abandoned, and annoyed that my father hadn't gotten me up. Yet I suppose if he had I'd have felt just as cranky since I had to face a whole day with Fern and her mother.

Nostalgically I thought of other Saturdays when my dad and I had had breakfast together. If he'd had school duties we'd plan our day for when he was free. We'd had such good times, just the two of us.

I took my time eating and getting dressed, and finally

went out to the ball field. Fern and her mother were sitting up on the benches with a few other parents who were probably visiting their kids for the day. My father was out on the field, and just as I came along Paul Rickenbacker made a beautiful stop. Everyone applauded. I would have liked to think that Paul was my boyfriend, but it wasn't quite true, although I often thought it was pretty close. He came around to my father's house a lot when I was there. I went to the movies with him once, and he kissed me good night when he brought me home. When my father teased me and called him my boyfriend I pretended to be annoyed, but secretly I liked thinking that maybe he was.

When Dad called time, Paul came over to say hello, and I introduced him to Fern and Ellen. "Mrs. Hopkins and my father are going to get married," I announced. "They'll be living here."

"What about you?" Paul asked. "You going to be here, too?" He was looking at me eagerly, wanting me to say yes.

"No." I shook my head. "I'm still a weekender."

"That's too bad. What about you?" he asked Fern. "You going to be living here?"

"I guess so. And go to school here." She had been watching us with those deep eyes of hers and now she gave Paul a sweeping glance, as if she were sizing him up. I could see the wheels turning around in her head, trying to decide if he was worth going after.

"That's good," Paul said.

In minutes they discovered that they were both in the eleventh grade, or juniors as they said around Lenox Hill; in five minutes they were talking a mile a minute. Mostly Paul was doing the talking, telling her about the classes and the teachers she'd have.

As she listened, Fern became transformed. Her pretty but blank face became animated and sparkling. She laughed,

21

crinkled up her nose, flashed her eyes, and kept looking at Paul as if he were telling her some fantastic story. It didn't take me long to figure out she was going for him, right in front of my eyes. I could have killed Paul for obviously taking in her line. "It's such a relief to know someone who'll be in my classes," she gushed. "I was so nervous. I hate coming into a new school, especially after classes have started; I feel so out of it. I hope you won't mind if I kind of hang on to you in the beginning."

"I sure won't mind," Paul said, grinning enthusiastically. "Just stick with me." They exchanged a look that spoke volumes.

So there it was: She'd been here less than twenty-four hours and already she'd picked out the one boy in the whole school of 372 students who I'd thought was going to be my boyfriend. If my father thought I was going to love having this boy snatcher for a sister, he was going to find out differently.

When we left the soccer field I could see Fern looking at the school with new eyes. And I could almost hear her thoughts: I'm going to be here, living on campus with all these fabulous boys, around 250 of them to only a little over a hundred girls. Wow!

We all spent the afternoon going around to antique shops looking fruitlessly for a chest of drawers that Fern liked. She and I were pretty quiet, on my part because I was still angry about Paul and, besides, I couldn't think of anything to say. After I told her that I liked her boots—stunning black leather with brass buckles—and her suede jacket, there was nothing left to say. Fern had that way of looking as if she were totally preoccupied with her own thoughts, and that they were more interesting than anything happening around her. Ellen chatted a lot, but my father doesn't talk much when he's driving, and in the shops he poked around by

22

himself. Once off in a corner, I managed to put my arm through his, and he grinned at me happily. "I hope you're as happy as I am," he whispered, squeezing my arm. "It's been so lonely. It's wonderful to have a family again. Maybe next year we'll switch things around and you'll live with us and spend weekends with your mother. I'll have to discuss it with Hester when the time comes, but would you like that?"

"What about school?"

"You'd go to Lenox Hill, of course."

"I don't know if I'll want to leave my class," I said, but that was not my main reason. I'd had ideas about living with my father, if I could bear to leave Mom except for weekends, but with them there—never!

At the dinner table that night I realized that the worst part of the whole business was that my father was different since they were there. My dad and I got along well because we let each other alone. I liked to watch TV while I ate and he liked to read, so often I took a tray to watch my show, and he sat at the kitchen table with his dinner and a book or the newspaper. It was nice that way. But now everything was so formal, including the food. Ellen had bought candles and put them on the table, along with a bowl of flowers in the middle so you couldn't see anybody. And the courses were like those at a banquet, with soup, a roast, two vegetables, salad, and a dumb dessert she called fruit compote. With Dad alone we'd make a hamburger or hot dogs or spaghetti and meatballs, and then go out to get ice cream if we wanted dessert. We ate real food, not fancy stuff. I wondered if he knew what he was getting into, eating that way every night and listening to Ellen say at least three times how glad she was that she'd bought the lamps at that antique shop, but maybe she should have gotten that pretty pine washstand.

My father had to remind her with a smile that she didn't buy it because she didn't know where she'd put it, but if she really wanted it, she could go back for it.

"You girls are so quiet," Ellen said after dinner. "Are you tired? What would you like to do? Do you have any games?" she asked, turning to my father.

"I'm afraid not. I'm not big on games. I went to a poker game over at Tim Harrington's once—he's one of the masters, teaches Latin—but it's not my cup of tea. What about a movie? What's playing, Amanda?"

"How should I know? I don't live here."

My father gave me a sharp look. "You can look in the paper," he said quietly.

"Fern has the paper," I told him. She had picked it up and was sitting on the sofa looking at the TV listings. My father had been arranging logs in the fireplace and now turned around. "Would you like to go to the movies?" he asked Fern.

"Not particularly. There's a good movie on TV."

That was the end of that. Naturally we stayed home and watched a dumb 1960 comedy that wasn't very funny. I went up to bed as soon as it was over, although my father asked if anyone wanted to go out for ice cream. No one was enthusiastic.

Sunday morning my father asked me to go with him to get the paper, and I knew I was in for a lecture. He didn't waste any time. We were hardly out of the driveway when he said, "I realize this is hard for you, Mandy, but I do think you might try a little more. This is not easy for Fern, either, and it worries her mother. Remember, Fern had to give up her friends in New York, move to a new school, and now start getting used to a new father. She was twelve years old when she lost her own father, and she was very attached to him. It hasn't been a cinch for Fern or her mother to get along on their own. Ellen happens to be a very gutsy lady. She hadn't worked when she was married, but when she was widowed she took a menial job in a department store because she needed the money." My father raced up to a STOP sign and then jammed on the brake. He's a good driver, but scary.

"I thought she believed in staying home," I said.

"Maybe she does, but she couldn't afford to. Now she will be able to stay home, and she's looking forward to it terribly. Life hasn't been easy for her, and I hope I can make it up to her. I want all three of you to be happy."

I couldn't bear seeing my father look almost teary and pleading. I'd never seen him that way before. Usually he had a wisecrack for everything. Even when he and my mom broke up he put on an act that it was best for everyone and not the end of the world. In fact, he made jokes about every kid having to go through at least one divorce these days or he or she'd be unconventional.

"I'll try," I said. But I couldn't help adding, "I wish you were marrying someone who didn't have any kids."

"But I'm not," he said tartly. "It happens that I fell in love with Ellen."

"I know." End of conversation. I hung on while he swerved around a curve.

It was a relief to get on the bus Sunday night. Usually saying good-bye was the worst. I hated saying good-bye to Mom on Friday morning before I went to school, and then saying good-bye to Dad on Sunday night, knowing I wouldn't see him all week. This had been going on for two years, yet I thought if I live to be a hundred, I'd never get used to it. But that Sunday, after dutifully kissing Ellen, letting Fern peck at my cheek, and throwing my arms around my father, I got onto the bus and prayed that it

25

would leave fast. Not only did I hate having to stay with Ellen and Fern another minute, but I didn't want to watch the three of them there, Ellen and Fern on either side of my father, waving at me and looking like a family. The people on the bus probably thought I was a girlfriend visiting Fern. I wondered what they'd have thought if they'd known that she was the outsider, not me.

When I got home I was so happy to see my mom I threw my arms around her and hugged her hard. She had on old jeans, her hair was mussed, and her face had some smudges on it. "What've you been doing?" I asked.

She waved toward the kitchen. "Trying to get that crummy paint off the cabinets. I discovered there's some fairly nice wood underneath."

The kitchen was a mess. "I bet you didn't wash a dish all weekend."

"Don't scold me. I didn't. I don't know how I ever had such a neat daughter. Just like my mother—I guess it skips a generation. Forget the kitchen, I'm dying to know about your weekend. What are they like?" My mother pulled me over to sit beside her on the sofa. "Is Mrs. Hopkins pretty?"

"Yes, very pretty. But I don't think you'd like her." I dug into the bag of potato chips my mother had beside her. Mom is an indifferent housekeeper. She does things like spending all weekend taking paint off a perfectly good cabinet and living in a mess of dirty dishes and cobwebs. I'm the one who always has to clean up after her.

"Of course I wouldn't like her. Without laying eyes on her I dislike her thoroughly. But you mustn't," she added hastily. "Why do you think I wouldn't like her?"

"She's not your kind. She's terribly neat," I said, looking around the room meaningfully, "and she likes to stay home. Dad's crazy about her."

26

"Maybe he'll get bored," she said. "Of course I hope he doesn't."

"I think you hope he does. Mom, why did you get divorced? Do you wish you were still married to Dad?" Although they had told me that they both wanted to separate, I had always thought it had been my mom's idea, but I didn't really know why.

My mom wriggled around as if trying to make herself comfortable. For someone who was usually so open with me, she had talked darn little about the divorce. Neither of my parents talked about their *feelings*—they pretended everything was okay even if you knew it wasn't.

"There was no *big* thing," my mother said. "Neither one of us was in love with anyone else. Maybe your father would have gone on the way we were—men are often resistant to making changes—but I wanted more than I was getting out of my life and out of a marriage if I was going to have one. We lost touch with each other; the content was gone. Living together became a burden instead of a pleasure. Maybe it was my fault, although I don't think it was anyone's fault. Your father is a good person, and I have nothing against him. But he's just not good for me."

"But I think you care that he's getting married again. Why should you?" I wanted her to care, to hate Ellen and Fern with me.

"I do and I don't. It's complicated. Objectively I don't— I'm glad for him. Yet I suppose there's some silly, childish part of me that resents his loving someone else. Maybe if I ever fall in love again I'll get over that, but honestly, I am happy for him. And you should be, too, I mean that. What's the girl like, your sister?"

"Don't call her my sister. She isn't and she never will be. She's a weirdo. She's pretty, like her mother, but to get a

27

smile out of her is worth your life. I think she hates me. She certainly hasn't gone out of her way to be friendly."

Trying to explain Fern was a pain. "She pretends to be real sophisticated, but I bet she isn't. She dresses like she's twenty. You should have seen her fluttering her eyes at Paul Rickenbacker. She's out to get him, to have a love affair with him. I hate her."

"What do you mean she's going to have a love affair? Girls of fifteen don't have love affairs. Who's Paul What's-his-name?"

"Paul Rickenbacker. I told you all about him. I went to the movies with him two weeks ago. You don't remember anything."

"Sorry. Do you like Paul?"

"Yes. And I'm sure Fern knew that, too. In fact, that's probably why she picked him. She's a boy stealer."

My mom laughed. "Amanda, you are funny. Come here." She pulled me to her and gave me a great hug. "Why do you hate Fern? You hardly know her, and I'm sure you're just imagining that she wants to steal Paul. Give her a chance. You are going to have to see a lot of her."

"That's what you think. I'm not going there next weekend." I hadn't even planned to say that—the words just came out. But once I said them, I knew that was exactly what I wanted to do. I was going to stay home.

"You can't do that, Mandy. I'm afraid you have to go. It's what your father and I agreed on."

"I don't care. You can't make me go. Dad was by himself when you made the agreement; now it's different. That agreement isn't good anymore."

Mom looked thoughtful. "Naturally I'd like to have you here for the weekend, but it's not right. I'd hate it if you decided you wanted to stay away from *me*." She shook her head "No, it wouldn't be fair to your father."

28

"He's not being fair to me. Why didn't he have me meet Ellen and Fern before he decided to marry them?"

"He's not marrying both of them," Mom said with a smile. "Besides, he doesn't need your approval. I think he has a right to assume that you will gracefully accept someone he loves." My mom stuffed her mouth with potato chips and lay back on the sofa pillows looking tired of the conversation. I never knew when she liked to talk about my dad and when she didn't. Sometimes she talked about him a lot and other times she changed the subject if I mentioned his name.

"I might accept Ellen, but that daughter of hers, never." Saying this, I got up and went to my room. It was an all right room but not as pretty as the one at my father's house. It looked out on the street and only got the sun for a little while in the morning, just the wrong time to wake me up. But I felt comfortable in it, and all my stuff was there—a few dolls I'd had since I was a baby, my books, posters of my favorite rock stars.

I sat down on my bed and looked out at the street. All of a sudden I got wildly angry at my parents, both of them. Why couldn't they have gotten along so I didn't have to live in two houses, have two separate birthdays, two Christmas celebrations, some things in one house and some in another? And now, to have to deal with a strange woman in one house and her stuck-up daughter, whom I knew I'd never like. People who got divorced shouldn't have children—but I knew it was too late for me not to be born. All I could do was be mad.

Chapter Four

It seems it took my mom a while to work herself up to a boil. When I came home from school Monday, she was fuming. "I've a good mind not to let you go to your father's next weekend," she said to me, after I'd kissed her and taken a soda from the fridge.

"That's a quick change. Yesterday you said it wasn't fair if I didn't go. What's up?"

"I've been thinking about it." She looked at me embarrassed, which was not like her. "I don't think it's right for that woman to be living in the same house with your father before they're married." She spoke defiantly, as if someone had been arguing with her. "Not with two young girls around."

I laughed. "Oh, Mom. Dad said they moved in now because they wanted Fern to get started in school and Ellen wanted to do some things in the house to prepare for the wedding. Besides, she has her own room. It's all very proper."

"I don't think it is. And I don't think your father should expose you to it. Anyway, *I* don't intend to."

I couldn't believe her, but she was serious. "Mom, that's crazy. They're going to be married in a couple of weeks; what difference does it make? What makes you such a Puritan all of a sudden? I've seen the way that man Craig looks at you with his sexy eyes."

My mom blushed. "You're impossible. If I ever do sleep with a man, I can assure you it won't be in this house where we are living together."

"I don't see what difference that makes. I think you're jealous that Dad's getting married again." I felt I had hit home.

"I certainly am *not* jealous," she said vehemently, but that made me all the more sure. "Besides, there is a difference. People's sex lives should be private, and parents should not involve their children in what they do. If your father wants to have premarital sex, that's his business, but his daughter, our daughter, doesn't have to know about it."

"You're getting all excited about nothing. I told you he put her in another room. Anyway, you don't have to worry about it, because I'm not going. You don't have to give me a reason."

"I intend to talk to your father," she said. She took some cutlets out of the fridge and started pounding them with a wooden mallet. My mother's a very good cook and I marvel at the meals she turns out of that messy kitchen. Although she says she's an artist, not a housekeeper, I suppose her creativity extends to food, too.

"Don't. Please, Mom, you'll make a big fuss about nothing. Besides, I don't want Dad to think I come back and report everything to you." I hated my parents to get into arguments. I knew I often told my mother too much about my dad and what we did together. She wanted to hear

31

everything, but after she did she either got depressed or found something to criticize about him, and then I wished I hadn't talked so much.

"This is strictly between your father and me. It has nothing to do with you, and I think you should keep out of it," my mother said.

I watched her flour and season the cutlets, trying to keep calm. I could tell by the look on her face that she was still fired up. If this was going to be a repeat of what had happened while my father wasn't teaching, I was determined to stop her. He had been working on a book about a divorced man living alone and his teenage daughter, but when I told my mother about it, she raised the devil. She called him and said he had no right to write a book about me, and if he tried to get it published she'd stop it. There was a great ruckus that made me feel terrible, and my dad finally dropped the idea. Mom is unpredictable. She can go along calmly, repeatedly telling me how lucky I am to have such a lovely man for a father—even though she couldn't live with him—and then all of a sudden blow her top about something he does. You never knew with her what was going to happen next.

"Mom, it *does* have to do with me," I said in my most reasonable voice. "If you make a fuss it will make things worse for me with Ellen and Fern. They'll think I'm just trying to make trouble. Please don't. Promise me you won't say anything to Dad."

"I'll have to think about it," she said stubbornly.

I decided it was best not to argue anymore. My mom is pretty broad-minded, so something had to be bugging her about my father. It was Mary who gave me the answer next day in school. In a way I had known it myself, but I didn't want to admit it.

"Your mother doesn't want to be married to your father,"

Mary said, "but she doesn't want anyone else to have him, either."

"That's not very nice," I said morosely. "It's not fair."

"Who's fair? Maybe your mother's still in love with him."

"Then why'd she want to get divorced?"

"Who knows? Grown-ups do crazy things. We're not the only ones," Mary added, sympathetically. "Maybe she just likes living alone better."

"She's not alone; she's got me."

"I mean without a man," Mary said. "I've decided it's a waste of time to try to figure out what grown-ups do. My mom's crazy about my father, at least she says she is, but you should hear the way she bawls him out for the most ridiculous things—like leaving his underwear on the floor instead of putting it in the hamper. You'd think he was committing a crime. I don't know why she doesn't just pick it up herself."

Mary looked so indignant I had to laugh. "Don't get yourself all worked up about it," I said.

She laughed. "I know. That's what I'm telling you."

We changed the subject then because Freddie Rich came over and sat down at our table in the cafeteria. "Am I interrupting a serious discussion?" he asked. Freddie's a brain. He knows more about computers than our teacher does, and he's been a ham radio buff since he was nine and talks to people all over the world. But he isn't stuck-up or spacey. He goofs off like everyone else and plays a great game of tennis.

"No," Mary told him. "We were just talking about Amanda's parents. Her father's getting married again."

"To a woman with a daughter a year and a half older than I am," I added.

"And you don't like it," Freddie said. "That figures. Do

you know that of the twenty-six kids in my class, only nine live with their own two parents who have never been divorced or remarried? I can give you more statistics if you want. Listen, kid, you're not alone. We're all in the same boat."

"I'll say," Mary remarked. "I don't ever intend to get married because I don't want to get divorced. It stinks."

"My mom says it's better than two people living together who don't love each other anymore."

"My mother's on her third husband," Freddie said. "I hope this one sticks."

"Do you like him?" I didn't think Freddie looked too happy.

"He's okay. Said he was going to take me on a fishing trip. We'll see. The last one was going to take me to California, but he never got around to it. Promises, promises."

"They all make promises," Mary said. Her parents had separated and come back together again. She was constantly worried that they were going to leave each other and stay that way.

It was a depressing conversation, but as usual we ended up laughing at each other's gloomy faces.

That night my father called to tell me that on Saturday we were all going down to Westchester to see Fern's grandparents. He telephoned because he wanted to be sure that I brought a skirt with me on Friday.

"You don't have to worry about my skirt," I said. "I'm not going. I can't come this weekend."

"What do you mean you can't come. Of course you're coming. Let me talk to your mother." He was angry before I even had a chance to give him a reason.

I called my mom to the phone and stood next to her,

34

listening. "I can't make her go," she said. "She's not a baby. Maybe she needs time getting used to her new relatives."

I couldn't hear what my father said, but I could see my mother's mouth tightening. She was getting mad. "Listen, David," she said, "you'll have to deal with this yourself. And don't accuse me of pushing her. I can't make her love your new wife and stepdaughter. And it's foolish of you to expect her to be deliriously happy. She was used to having you to herself on weekends, so this is bound to be hard on her."

I thought she was going to hang up on him, but she handed the phone back to me. "He wants to talk to you again."

This time my father was pleading. "Consider it a favor to me," he said. "Mr. and Mrs. Shane, Ellen's parents, are really eager to meet you. They are making quite elaborate preparations, I understand. Everyone would be very disappointed. The whole thing was arranged for the two of us— don't leave me in the lurch. Please, Amanda."

I couldn't say no after that. But I wasn't happy about it. Every day, it seemed, things got worse. I hadn't counted on Ellen and Fern having a family. That meant a whole bunch of new relatives to visit besides all my mother's and my father's. Ever since the divorce my grandparents and aunts and uncles acted like I was an orphan without a home and kept wanting me to come visit them. I had to explain to them that I had *two* homes and between that and school and basketball practice and rehearsals for plays and sometimes wanting to see my own friends, I couldn't go traveling around all over. And now this.

"So what are you going to do?" my mother asked when I hung up the receiver.

"I guess I'm going. What are you going to do about Ellen living there?"

Our eyes met and my mother gave an embarrassed laugh. "I guess nothing. I don't suppose it makes any difference." But she looked sad as she turned away.

With my arms around her I asked, "Are you still in love with Daddy?"

She hugged me back and then squirmed away. "No, I'm not in love," she said. "But we were married, and we had you, and it's sad to know that we can both have other lives. I didn't think that either one of us could ever love anyone else, but it seems that we can. When I was your age I thought that you fell in love and that you stayed that way for the rest of your life. It's painful to discover that that's not always the case. But you can still care about someone without being in love. I never could understand people who felt they had to hate each other because they got divorced."

"What makes people fall out of love?" By now we were sitting on a step between our living room and the two bedrooms. Our apartment was in an old, remodeled, two-family house, and there were different levels where walls had been broken through.

"It's not one thing, and it's hard to know. Maybe we got married too young, and we've grown up differently. We tried, Amanda . . . neither one of us wanted to hurt the other. I think we're both decent, caring people, but we started to get on each other's nerves, to become irritating and irritated. I wasn't willing to settle for that, and I don't think David really was, either. I want more and so does he. I hope he finds it with Ellen. I honestly do."

He won't, I thought to myself, but I didn't say so out loud. I felt confused and terribly sad. Everything seemed so pointless to me. My parent's wedding picture was still sitting on top of the bookcase. It had been there ever since I could remember. They looked so happy, so terribly young and full of hope. I'd heard everything my mother had said, that they irritated each other, that they'd drifted apart, but it was hard to connect all that with the couple in the photograph. Why would my father get along better with Ellen than he did with my mother? To me my mom was a superior person. "Why do you think he's going to be better off with Ellen?" I asked.

My mother looked surprised. "Maybe he's learned from our experience. He's older now, and from what you say, I suspect Ellen is very different from me. Your father's a bright man, and I think intellectually he believes a woman should be independent. But at the same time he wants and needs a lot of attention, and maybe I didn't give him enough. I hope he can get it from her. When we married, I was very dependent on him. I let him make all the decisions. But that changed when I went to work and started to earn my own money. I wish you didn't have to deal with all this," she said, impatiently turning around to face me. "I hate making you unhappy."

It's too late now, I thought. Out loud, I only said I had to go do my homework. But with so many thoughts chasing around in my head it was hard to concentrate on the rights and wrongs of the Civil War, a paper I had to write for social studies.

Saturday morning at my father's house we had to get up early for the drive to Westchester. I put on the new wool skirt my mother had insisted on buying so that I'd look "smashing," as she said, and a cashmere sweater of hers she had spent a fortune on. Ellen immediately took note of the sweater when I came down for breakfast.

"It's my mother's," I told her.

"Your mother has good taste," she said, looking at my father for his approval. "It's a very pretty sweater."

"Hester spends all her money on clothes," my father said, without turning around from the stove where he was scrambling eggs. He prides himself on his scrambled eggs.

"That's not true," I said. "She buys good things but she only buys them once in a while. She hasn't got a lot of clothes."

"I wasn't criticizing your mother," my father said. "You don't have to defend her."

"Maybe I do," I mumbled.

"Here are your eggs. Sit down." My father gave me a look that said, Don't make trouble. "I'd like to get started as early as possible," he added.

"Where's Fern?"

"She had her breakfast; she's outside," my father told me.

I looked out the window and there she was sitting on the stone wall, talking to Paul Rickenbacker. I was right: She had gone after him, and she'd won. He was sitting next to her, laughing and talking. They looked like an ad in a magazine—all they needed was an open sports car beside him. I lost my appetite for my father's super eggs. I was glad when Ellen called Fern in to get ready to go.

I think Fern's grandparents lived to eat. When we got there we'd barely said hello before Mrs. Shane brought out a huge plate of coffee cake, sandwiches, and coffee; milk or juice for Fern and me. While everyone was eating, she talked about lunch. "I fixed a smorgasbord," she said. "I wanted to be sure there would be some things my new granddaughter likes. When I get to know her better I can have her special favorites, just the way I have Fern's black olives and artichoke hearts. Heaven forbid I shouldn't have them when she comes," she said with a laugh.

Mrs. Shane was small and plump and laughed a lot, more than her husband, who looked as if he did the worrying for the family. My mother would have been critical of their house—it had so many things around. Lots of lamps, shelves with glass animals, plates on the walls, hanging plants, tables covered with assorted boxes, and bowls of artificial fruit. I was afraid to walk around for fear I'd accidentally knock something over.

We spent most of the day eating; the food was fantastic. Fern seemed bored most of the time, while Ellen occupied herself carrying dishes back and forth from the kitchen. I got along fine with Mrs. Shane, though. She told me more than once that she was going to love me just the same as Fern. "No difference," she said. "You'll be my grand-daughter the same as she is."

When I told her that I had two grandmothers already, she simply laughed and said that now I'd have a third one. The only problem was that she kept forgetting my name. One minute she called me Amanda, then Arlene, then Amy.

The strangest part of the day was seeing my father in that setting. Dad is a large man and he likes a lot of space. Usually he sits with his legs stretched out in front of him and they go a long way. But the Shane house was so crowded with furniture that my poor father looked comical trying to get comfortable. I wanted to laugh everytime I saw him squirming around, or standing up to stretch.

It was a peculiar day because there didn't seem to be much time for people to talk, although I think my father had some conversation with Mr. Shane. The food kept us all busy. The lunch wasn't a lunch but a seven-course meal: Mrs. Shane's idea of a smorgasbord was two soups, three different kinds of meat, jellies and pickles, a million salads, cheeses, fruits, and cakes. Then she brought out candy, more fruit, and cookies. Naturally I stuffed myself some more, which made Mrs. Shane very happy.

We left around five o'clock, and my father was driving up the Parkway when I began to feel woozy. I tried to think of other things, to concentrate on not getting sick, when Fern, who was sitting next to me in the back, yelled, "Please stop the car. I've got to get out."

My father pulled off the road onto some grass, and the next thing I knew Fern and I were being sick behind some bushes. It was horrible. Ellen and my father had come out of the car after us, but we waved them away. Tears were running down our cheeks when we finished. We both looked a mess. "Oh, boy, was I sick," Fern said. "A good thing my grandmother didn't see this. She'd feel hurt."

"I know. I made a pig of myself."

"Me, too. I always eat too much at her house. There's nothing else to do."

When we looked at each other, we laughed.

She's human, I thought. Maybe I hadn't really looked at her before. All of a sudden she was like someone I could possibly talk to without thinking she was going to ruin my life. If throwing up with someone was a way to break the ice, I was grateful to her grandmother for stuffing us with all that food.

Once we got back into the car, though, Fern seemed to close up again. She shut her eyes, and I think she was dozing off when Ellen turned around and said, "You shouldn't have eaten the shrimp salad, Fern. You always get sick from shrimp."

"I do not. That's not what made me sick. I just ate too much."

"I don't think so. It was the shrimp," her mother repeated.

40

"You don't know what makes me sick," Fern said, and for some reason, I got the feeling she was talking about a lot of things other than food. "I'm tired. If you don't mind, I'm going to sleep." She curled up on her side of the car and closed her eyes again.

For the first time I felt a wave of sympathy, or maybe I felt sorry for Fern. Her face had a crumpled look as if she were hurting even in her sleep and that made me think there was a lot about her that I didn't know. Despite the hint of friendship and the bond we'd shared just a few minutes ago, I wondered if I would ever really get to know her and if we could be friends.

Chapter Five

There was only one more weekend before the wedding, and I was glad to get that one over with. You'd think the royal couple was getting married. Ellen had decided the downstairs hall needed painting, so my father was busy with that the whole weekend. I didn't have any time with him at all, and wished I hadn't come. I don't know why he wanted me to. When I said as much to him, he got a hurt look on his face and said I was part of a family and not to behave like a spoiled baby.

I was in the hall with him when he said that, and of course Fern came in at just that moment and heard him. She went right out but I caught a satisfied look on her face, as if she were glad to see me put down by my dad. But I had my turn later.

She was in the kitchen with her mother and she was getting scolded for helping herself to a bowl of berries Ellen was planning to use for dessert after supper. "I thought I was supposed to feel at home here," Fern was saying. "How should I know you wanted to save the berries."

"You might have asked," her mother said.

"I didn't think I had to ask for permission to eat something," Fern said haughtily.

Ellen looked near tears. "You're not being very helpful. I thought you'd be very happy here." Realizing a lot more was going on than an argument about berries, I quickly went out without getting the soda I'd wanted, but not before Fern gave me a cold stare that told me I was intruding.

That week went no better than the weekend had. I flunked two exams in school and was warned that I'd better shape up.

And then, the weekend of the wedding.

On Saturday, the day before the big event, Fern and I went out to do some shopping. We both needed to get out of the house. There was a lot of activity at home, where the ceremony and a luncheon reception were going to be held. Ellen kept saying it was to be a simple, small affair, but it didn't look that way to me. My father's house was filling up with flowers; the caterers had started bringing tables, chairs, and dishes early Saturday morning; Ellen was polishing silver; and my father was, of all things, waxing the floor. They had nothing for us to do, and, I think, we both felt in the way.

Fern wanted to buy a pair of slacks, I needed shoes, and it was an excuse to walk around the shopping mall. When we left the house I started to walk on the road down the hill to the village, but Fern said to follow her. She cut across someone's lawn, behind a few houses, and took a path through the woods.

"How'd you find this?" I asked, amazed.

"I find things," she said. "It's shorter." She'd only been here a few weeks, but she knew her way around.

In the store she kept amazing me. She tried on about a dozen pair of slacks and piled them up on the floor of the dressing room before she found a pair that suited her. And then she asked the saleslady to get her a fresher-looking belt, and to sew up a seam that had come apart. I was as nervous as a cat that the saleslady would get tired of this and throw us out, but Fern acted like she was a princess. I had to admire her cool.

While she was in the dressing room, she asked me to bring her some scarves she'd seen on a shelf. I brought in four she asked for, and she posed before the mirror trying each one around her head or shoulders. I waited by the cash register while she got dressed, and then she joined me to pay for her slacks.

"Didn't you buy any of the scarves?" I asked.

"No, they're too expensive."

But when we were a few blocks away she pulled a fabulous silk scarf out from inside her blouse. "How'd you get that?" I asked dumbly.

"I took it, what do you think? I wasn't going to pay twenty dollars for a scarf. It's pretty, isn't it?"

"You mean you *stole* it?" I was shocked.

"If that's what you want to call it. They had dozens— they won't miss it. They mark things up so high it doesn't matter. It's not as if they're poor." She put the scarf into her bag. "You're not a tattletale, are you?" She looked at me intently.

"No, I won't say anything." I felt confused. I didn't know what to think or to say. I think she wanted to shock me, and she did. I'd never known anyone before who stole, and now here was someone who was going to be part of my family.

Fern acted perfectly natural, and I wondered if this was something she did all the time. I wished she hadn't told me because I didn't know how to deal with it. It made me feel uneasy and embarrassed.

We spent the rest of the day hanging around, trying to help in the house now that the caterers had left. Fern was the same as usual, but the thought of that scarf kept burning in my mind. Once, when my father admired a flower arrangement she made, I was dying to say, "You should only know the kind of thief she is! First Paul and now this."

Sunday was a perfect fall day—a beautiful day for a wedding. As soon as I woke up, it hit me: This was it, it was really going to happen. In one of my many fantasies I had imagined my father discovering some terrible secret about Ellen—I didn't bother to figure out what—and the whole thing would be called off. Dad would be brokenhearted for a while, but I would be there close to console him. . . . Poor, dopey Amanda with her foolish dreams. Lying in bed I could hear the house noises, already some activity in the kitchen. I supposed the caterers were back, this time bringing the food with them. Okay, I thought, it's a day I have to get through. I hugged my pillow to me—by the time I came back to bed that night it would all be over with, finis.

The trouble was I couldn't even enjoy feeling miserable; I felt guilty. A wedding was a happy event—my father was happy, and I should be happy with him. I went over in my mind all the positive things I could think of: I had my mom, my friends at home, my stereo and records and tapes, my bike; I would at least *see* my dad (he wasn't moving to some foreign country); I might go to camp next summer; and someday my father would find out what kind of girl Fern was. I got up feeling better.

When I went across the hall to go to the bathroom, I saw Fern in her mother's room. The door was partly open, and her mother was sitting on the edge of the bed holding Fern's head in her lap. Fern was crouched on the floor, and while I couldn't see her face, I had the feeling that she was crying. I walked past quickly. When I came out of the bathroom they were both standing up, and Ellen saw me walk by. She was still holding her daughter close, and she met my eyes over Fern's head.

"Fern's a little upset today," Ellen said, gesturing me to come in. "She and her father were very close, and it's hard for her to see me marrying someone else. Although I know she's glad to see me happy."

Fern pulled her face away from her mother, and I could see that she had been crying. I also had a strong feeling that she was furious that her mother had allowed me to see her this way and to hear about her feelings for her father.

"I'm okay," Fern said brusquely. "Don't worry about me."

Ellen sighed and mumbled something like she would always worry about her daughter. I wanted to get away so I said I'd better go get dressed. I felt that I had been shown something I shouldn't have seen, and felt a momentary bond with Fern. Or maybe it was feeling sorry for her again. She was as miserable as I. The difference was she didn't have a mom like mine to turn to.

It is pretty strange to be at your father's wedding. I kept wishing my mother was there, which was crazy. But if she had been I would have had someone to giggle with, especially when the minister got mushy and spoke about enduring love, the responsibilities of marriage, and stuff like that. After all, it wasn't as if my father and Ellen were kids getting married for the first time. They probably knew more about being married than he did.

I felt silly standing up with them, afraid to look at my father for fear I might get weepy. It was peculiar how that whole day I felt on the verge of either tears or a fit of giggles. Fern and I wore dresses that were alike, pale pink cotton with long, full skirts and fitted tops. But Fern filled out her top, while mine was flat and childish looking.

There were a lot of people, and after the ceremony, tons of good food. My father even let me have a glass of champagne. He insisted on taking me around and introducing me to everyone—Ellen's friends and relatives, and people from the school—although I knew I'd never remember any names and probably not see most of them again. Fern's grandmother wanted to do the same thing. I had a terrible time getting her to understand that my father had already introduced me, but she went right on, dragging me around the room anyway.

After spending a little time with my father's few relatives and some old friends of his whom I knew, I went up to my room. I wanted to be alone. But I wasn't there very long before my father came up after me.

"What's the matter? Are you okay?" he asked.

"Yes, sure. Why shouldn't I be?"

"No reason. But what are you doing up here?" He had come over to where I was sitting at my desk, looking out the window, and sat down on the edge of the desk.

"I just felt like it."

He was looking at me with troubled eyes, and I was about to put my arms around him when Ellen walked in. She wasn't dressed as a bride with a veil and all, but she looked very pretty in a long white dress of some thin material with bands of lace on the skirt. "Oh, here you are." She came over to my father and put her arm around his shoulder. "Anything the matter?" She looked from him to me.

She seemed to be asking me, so I shook my head. "No, what should be the matter? I just came up here for a few minutes."

"It seemed an odd thing to do, when the party's

downstairs," my father said. "Are you coming down soon?" He sounded formal, not like himself.

"Of course she is," Ellen said, putting her other arm around me. "It's a happy day. We're going to be very good friends, Amanda and I. I'm not going to try to be a mother to you, Mandy, you have a mother, but we will be friends. I know we will."

Don't say it, I thought to myself, please don't say it, because if you do, it will never happen. Besides, I wished she hadn't come up. My dad and I might have been alone together a bit—I'd have liked that.

After I assured them again that I was okay, they left me and went downstairs. I turned back to the window and saw Fern standing out in back by herself. It had turned cool and she had thrown on one of my father's sweaters that hung in the hall. It was miles too big for her and she looked small and huddled in it. I thought she looked lonely and unhappy, and for a minute I wondered if I should go down and be with her. But then, while I was watching, she picked up some stones and started to hurl them, one after another, at a big black birch tree in the backyard. She was throwing them hard, as if the tree was something or someone she really wanted to hurt. If she had been aiming at someone, those stones would have knocked that person out; I wondered who she had in mind. She frightened me. I kept seeing private sides to her that were scary and so different from the cool, controlled way she behaved when people were around.

It was after eight o'clock by the time all the guests had left and the caterers had cleaned up downstairs. Ellen had taken off her wedding dress and was going around in a housecoat, and my father had gotten into jeans and a sweater. Fern and I still had on our dresses. All four of us were sitting around the living room not saying much. It seemed strange.

"Aren't you two going to do something to celebrate?" I asked my father and his new wife.

Ellen laughed. "We've been celebrating all day." She was on the sofa next to my father, her head against his shoulder. "I think we're all tired."

"I thought people went off on honeymoons."

"People do," my father said, "but that doesn't mean we will. It's back to work tomorrow as usual. Maybe we'll go someplace later, during vacation. We don't need a honeymoon." His arm tightened around Ellen, and he kissed her hair.

I didn't think people *needed* a honeymoon, I just thought they wanted one. Had he wanted one with my mother? She had told me many times about the canoe trip she and my father had taken for a honeymoon. It had sounded terribly romantic, paddling across lakes in Maine, sleeping under the stars, and stopping at farm houses for food. They had been so much in love—I couldn't connect her stories with my father now, sitting with his arm around a middle-aged woman who didn't look like she would ever want to get into a canoe.

Ellen stood up abruptly and picked up a bowl of wilting flowers.

"What are you doing? I thought you were tired." My father looked at her lovingly.

"I can't stand these dead flowers. I'm just going to throw them away." Ellen walked out of the room with my father following her with his eyes. Fern had been sitting on the floor and now stretched out on her stomach, putting her head on her arms. She's going to ruin her dress, I thought, but I didn't say anything.

Ellen came in and settled back on the sofa, but the room wasn't peaceful anymore. There were tensions I felt but didn't understand. After a while, Fern lifted her head and

49

asked her mother if she could move her things into the study Ellen had been using.

"You can do it tomorrow," her mother said. "There's plenty of time."

"No, I'll do it tonight," Fern said. She walked out of the room and we heard her going upstairs.

Then I remembered that Ellen would be moving in with my father and I suddenly thought, I bet Fern doesn't like that any more than I do. But it wasn't Fern who was on my mind, it was Ellen and my father, snuggled up against each other. I remembered once hearing a friend of my mother's say that my dad was a very attractive man. I had never thought of him in terms of sex, or as a sexual person, the way I had in daydreams about Paul. When he used to walk around the house with a towel draped over his middle I teased him because he looked comical, and when I was little and used to crawl into the big bed with him and my mother, it wasn't sexy, just warm and comforting.

But now, watching him absently stroking Ellen's arm, I felt terribly conscious of the fact that they were going to go upstairs and sleep together. It was a peculiar feeling because I was embarrassed. I had never felt that way when he and my mother had gone off to their bedroom together—I hadn't given it too much thought. Maybe it was because I was younger then. With Ellen it was different. She was a more overtly sexy woman than my mother. She was like a cat rubbing herself against him and purring, and my father suddenly appeared very physical.

I felt that I needed familiar arms around me for comfort—all that was going on between the two of them was a mystery I didn't want to know about. I got lonesome for my mother. "Can I call up Mom?" I asked my father.

His face closed up the way it did whenever I talked about my mother. "You'll see her tomorrow," he said.

"I know. But I want to talk to her now. It's not so expensive; I won't talk long."

"I wasn't thinking of the money."

"Then why can't I?"

He glanced at Ellen and then back at me. Her face was trying to be expressionless, but I could tell she was very concerned with the conversation. "Because this is time you're spending here. I don't have to give you a reason," he added irritably.

"If she wants to call her mother, let her," Ellen said. "Stopping her doesn't help."

I looked to my father for his okay. "If you must, go ahead," he said reluctantly.

Walking out of the room I could hear him tell Ellen, "I think it's better if you keep out of this. Don't misunderstand me, I want you to be involved, but . . ." I didn't hear the rest.

My mom was home when I called. At first she sounded alarmed, but when I assured her there was nothing the matter, she wanted to know all about the wedding. I told her about the minister giving them advice, and how weird it was, and all about the people and the food. She giggled a lot and said that she missed me, but hoped I was having a good time.

Talking to her made me feel better, and I felt sorry for Fern who didn't seem to have any fun at all with her mother.

Chapter Six

Because of the wedding I didn't go home on Sunday night, but missing school on Monday was no big deal. I didn't tell my father I had a paper due that I hadn't written, so I was glad to have another day to do it.

Monday morning at breakfast I listened to the three of them making plans for the week and Fern and my father talk about things that were happening in the school. My father was urging her to try out for a play that was going to be performed sometime between Thanksgiving and Christmas.

"You'll like Meg Haley, the drama coach," he said. "She's young and bouncy, and I've been told she's very good. She's worked in summer theater."

"I'll think about it," Fern said.

"Why are you hesitating?" her mother asked. "You love acting and your father thinks you'd enjoy it."

Fern gave her mother a startled look. "He's not my father," she murmured in a low voice, although we all heard her.

There was an awkward silence for a few seconds. "I'd

like to be," my father said with the kind of smile he used when he wanted me to do something I didn't like. "As a matter of fact, your mother and I were discussing a legal adoption, but we don't have to talk about that right now." He gave me a quick glance and turned back to his eggs. "There's plenty of time."

It was happening. This was worse than her taking over Paul. Dad *was* being her father, and they were weaving a whole life together. He was even going to make it legal. In my worst moments I never thought it would happen so fast, that a complete stranger could walk into his life and, presto, become his daughter. I felt as if I were living in someone else's story. This couldn't be happening to me, that my own father would want, would accept, another daughter so easily. Perhaps I was a fool to think that he had ever really loved me.

"Do you still want to see that movie we talked about?" my father asked Fern. "I think on Wednesday we could make the early show."

I asked which movie, and of course it was the one I was dying to see. "Can't you wait for the weekend?" I asked.

"Thursday's the last night," my father said. "Maybe you can catch it with your mother."

"Probably not," I said, feeling totally deflated.

Fern and my father went on talking about some of the masters, the kids in Fern's class, and an upcoming basketball game. Dad tried to get me to talk but I didn't care about what was going on in Lenox Hill, and certainly not in Fern's classes.

"I've got to go and get my bus," I said, although I had more than half an hour. I preferred waiting down at the bus stop to sitting there listening to them.

"I'll walk down with you," my father said.

I was ready for another lecture, but he was quiet on the

walk. His mind seemed preoccupied. He only said that he hoped I'd have a good week, and that he knew things would work out. He didn't say what things, but I guess he meant my getting along with Ellen and Fern. But now that creep was stealing my father.

Tuesday, at school, Mr. Adams was all ready to bawl me out for handing in my paper late, but when I explained about my father's getting married he softened up. However, later in the day he stopped me in the hall and said he'd like to talk to me after school, and would I come to his classroom. I'm crazy about Mr. Adams—everyone is. He teaches English literature and gives a special class in American writers for advanced students that's really neat. It's a small class and we talk about everything. Mr. Adams and his wife have a new baby, and it's funny the way he manages to bring stories about his baby into the discussion. We tease him about that. He thinks it's pretty funny, too.

I wasn't worried about seeing him, so right after the last bell I went to his classroom. I saw that he had my paper on top of his desk. He greeted me and motioned me to sit down.

He picked up my paper and glanced at it and then at me. He looked serious. "What's happened to you, Amanda?" he asked.

"What do you mean?" I didn't know what he was talking about.

"You've been such a good student. I can't believe you would turn in a paper like this."

"What's the matter with it? I thought it was pretty good." The paper was about *Ethan Frome*, a book I'd read and thought terrific.

"I don't know what made you think so. Did you read it after you wrote it?"

"Maybe not."

"I suggest you do. I won't even talk about the spelling, your handwriting, and the sentence structure. They're terrible. But I could forgive that if the paper made sense. It's positively incoherent. What's the matter? Are you thrown by your father's marriage? Is that bothering you?"

"Maybe." I didn't feel like talking about it. Not even to Mr. Adams.

"People get married, you know. Don't hold it against your father because he's fallen in love with someone. I'm sure she's very nice, and you'll get to be great friends."

"I don't need any friends." I sounded sullen. I was so sick of everyone telling me we were going to be great friends. "Are you going to give me an *F*?"

"I'm afraid I have to. Read it, you'll see why. I could let you write it over if you want."

"I don't want to. It probably wouldn't be any better." I couldn't stand the thought of rewriting it. "I'll do better next time."

"I hope so. I hope you feel better, too."

"Can I go now?" I stood up and took the paper he handed me. The way he was looking at me I was afraid I'd burst into tears. I can't stand people feeling sorry for me.

I went outside, and, wouldn't you know it, some kid went by on a bike and spattered mud all over my jeans. That was the end. I ran back into school, locked myself in the girls' room, and burst into tears. I really cried, while at the same time trying to be quiet. I'd have died if anyone came along and heard me.

After I stopped and washed my face, I went outside again and walked over to the ice-cream parlor where Mary and I usually went for a soda. She was there, thank goodness, sitting with Freddie.

I felt so good seeing them. They are my true friends, I

thought, they know me and care about me—they don't make me feel awkward and stupid. Impulsively I gave Mary a hug. She knew immediately that I needed her, and she gave me a bear hug back. Even Freddie, who's not as perceptive as Mary, understood, because he didn't make any wisecracks about our being emotional.

Mary had the sense not to ask me any questions. Although Freddie's a good friend, there are things we don't talk about in front of him. Boys are different. There are feelings they don't understand or they laugh at; not to be mean, but because they react differently, I think. Anyway, having a soda with them and talking about nothing in particular made me feel better. I am sorry for anyone who doesn't have friends. When you're feeling down or are in trouble, friends are the only ones who can cheer you up.

But that was not my day. When I got home my mother was gloomy. She'd gotten a phone call from my homeroom teacher. "They're worried about you at school," she said. "Social studies, math, Spanish, which you love—I'm told you're not paying attention, your mind always seems to be someplace else, and you're not doing your work. What's the matter?" She looked worried. Usually my mother doesn't care too much about high marks. She says that what you learn day by day is more important than exams. But this time she was upset. "I know you're going through a rough time, but even so."

"What rough time? People get married; lots of people do. If you think I'm upset about that, forget it." I felt perverse. I knew I was doing rotten in school, but I wasn't going to admit that it had anything to do with my father, Ellen, or Fern.

My mother smiled. "You're not fooling me, Mandy. You don't have to be ashamed about being upset. It's only natural. Oh, dear, I have a date with Craig tonight. We're going to dinner and to a concert. But I could break it and we could do something together, or just stay here and talk. Would you like that?"

"You don't have to break a date because of me. I'm okay, honest."

My mother cupped my face between her hands and studied it.

"I'm really all right," I repeated. "Can't we get rid of this rug? It's so ugly." The whole room looked shabby. Compared to my father's house it was a dump. The slipcovers made to hide the old sofa already had holes, and the two chairs were so worn down that it was like sitting in a basin. "You ought to fix this place up."

"What for? Maybe, if it means that much to you, and a big job comes through, I will."

"Ellen's fixing up Dad's house. She's buying a new rug."

"Good for her. I don't see anything wrong with this one. I spend my money, when I have it, on other things. Is she rich?"

"No. Dad says she's not. But he makes money, doesn't he?"

"Teachers don't make a lot of money, especially in private schools. He has his rent free, which helps. Would you rather be living with your father and his new rug?"

The question took me by surprise. I couldn't tell by my mother's solemn brown eyes if she was serious. My father used to call my mother an imp because of the way she looks with her short black hair and large almond-shaped eyes that are usually laughing. I love it when people tell me I look like her, because she's fantastic.

"No, of course not. I don't mind about the rug and the old furniture, but what about Craig? He's so elegant."

Mom laughed. "He'd love to hear that. Anyway, I don't think he gives a darn about our furniture."

"He loves you for yourself, I know." I was teasing, but she blushed and I got scared. What if she got married, too? That would be too much to handle at once.

I wanted to stay up in my room when Craig came, but Mom insisted I be downstairs. She said she liked to show off her beautiful daughter, but I had a feeling she wanted me to get to like him. Craig is good-looking, in an arty sort of way, I have to admit that. He's tall and slim and wears his hair rather long. He's got a big nose but it goes with the rest of his face. He's got some gray in his hair, his eyebrows are quite gray, and his deepset eyes look at you as if they're seeing right into you.

I think he's embarrassed with me. He asked me how I was and how school was going, and while he was talking to me he walked around the room fidgeting. He picked up a book and put it down without looking at it. Mom told me he's never been married and has no kids, so I guess he doesn't know how to talk to one.

I didn't know how to talk to him, either. Someone should write a book telling kids how to talk to their parents' dates, new wives, and boyfriends. In the old days I bet it was easier when parents stayed married to each other forever. I don't know what I'd do if my mother decided to marry Craig. I can't imagine having a new father here day and night. At least I don't have to live with Ellen all the time.

"Did you have a good time at your father's wedding?" Craig asked.

What a dumb question, but I could tell he was racking his brain for something to say. "It was okay. Terrific food."

He laughed. "That's always a help." I bet he wanted to ask me more about my father but didn't have the nerve. He looked terribly relieved when Mom said she was ready to go. She looked fabulous in a black dress and loose purple coat, and I could tell he was admiring her.

"When you finish your homework you can watch TV if you want, but bed by ten o'clock. Remember, it's a school night." She kissed me goodnight and they left.

There was some barbecued chicken and salad in the fridge, so I took a plate of food into the living room to watch TV while I ate. The program was a silly sitcom, and my mind kept wandering. I thought about Mr. Adams and how I'd love to give him a super paper that he would get excited about.

But when I went upstairs to do my homework I couldn't keep my mind on it. The idea of doing a great paper was one thing, but writing it was another. Besides, I had to do math, and that was boring. I was like Craig, getting up and moving around the room, brushing my hair, going to the bathroom, suddenly straightening out my top drawer. Everything but doing my homework. I just couldn't concentrate. I thought about my mom and Craig; I wondered what my father and Ellen and Fern were doing; I tried to decide if Fern was seeing a lot of Paul Rickenbacker, then concluded she had to be since they were in classes together.

I had just sat down at my desk again when the phone rang. It was my father. He'd called to say hello and asked me about school. Then he said he wanted to talk to my mother.

"She's not here," I told him. "She went out."

"She's out? Are you alone?"

"Yes, of course. Why?"

"When will she be home?"

"Probably late. She went out on a date." You're not the only one, I felt like adding.

"Did you have anything to eat?"

59

"Of course. I just finished a little while ago. What's the matter, you sound funny."

"I'm not funny." His voice was angry. "I don't like your being left alone. To have your dinner alone, and be alone all evening. Does this happen often?"

"I don't know; I don't count. I'm perfectly okay. I don't mind."

"*I* mind. Ask your mother to call me when she gets home."

"It will be late."

"I don't care. I'll be interested to know how late. Don't open the door to anyone, you hear. Finish your homework and go to bed."

After he hung up I sat by the phone. There was going to be a fight, I knew it. I should have lied and said she'd be home soon. But when she didn't call back right away he'd know, so that wouldn't have done any good.

I couldn't bear their having a fight about me. I wondered if they'd fought about me before and I didn't know it. Perhaps I was the reason they had gotten divorced. Mom used to tell me about what fun they'd had when she and my dad were going together. They didn't have much money, she said, and they were both still in college, but they went on hikes and picnics, and once took a cross-country skiing trip and got caught in a blizzard. They stayed in a farmhouse in Vermont, and she said they had the best meal they'd ever eaten for only two dollars apiece. The farm lady wouldn't take more because she told them they were young and in love and they cheered her up. Maybe if I hadn't been born they would have stayed in love.

I went back to my room after speaking to my dad, but if I had had a hard time concentrating before, it was impossible now. I got undressed and into bed, but going to sleep was out of the question. I kept listening for my mother to come home, which was silly as it wasn't even ten o'clock. I guess I dozed off a few times, but every time I looked the clock had hardly moved.

When it crept to one o'clock and she still wasn't home, I began to worry and get nervous. Maybe my dad was right and I shouldn't be alone in the apartment. We were on the street floor and it would be easy for someone to climb in a window. The more I thought about it, the more scared I got, and angry at my mother. She was the one who wanted me to live with her, so she had no business going off on a date and leaving me alone all night. Yet I didn't want to live with my father and his new family. I buried my face in my pillow and pulled the blanket over my head. If a burglar came in and murdered me, it would serve them all right.

I was lost in self-pitying thoughts when I heard the outside door open. I flew out of my room and saw Craig and my mother in the hallway, close up against one another. Craig had his arms around my mom and he was kissing her. They kissed for a long time while I stood silently in my nightgown watching them. When my mother lifted her head she saw me and gave a startled cry.

"Amanda, what are you doing?" She looked at me accusingly. "That's not a nice thing to do."

"I wasn't spying on you."

"What are you doing here in the middle of the night?" She had stepped away from Craig, who was looking at me with amusement.

"It's *not* the middle of the night. It's almost two in the morning."

"What are you doing, scolding me for coming home late?" Now she looked as if she was about to laugh.

"I don't care when you come home. But Dad does. He wants you to call him."

"Now? What for? Has something happened?"

"I don't think so. He said for you to call him whenever you came home. I told him it would be late, but he said he didn't care."

My mother frowned. "I don't think you're telling me the whole story, but I have no intention of calling him now. I'll talk to him tomorrow."

"He'll be mad."

"That's too bad." She turned to Craig. "It was a wonderful evening and I'm sorry you had to listen to all this." She gave him a helpless look that was not like my mom. He ate it up.

"Don't be silly. I'm concerned about you, about Amanda. Remember what I told you tonight." They looked at each other solemnly and he took her two hands in his. "Wait until tomorrow to call and get a good night's sleep. What there is left of the night, anyway." He bent down and kissed her again, waved his hand to me, and took off.

"You're not going to call?" I asked.

"No, I'm not. Go on up to bed; you have to get up for school in the morning."

"Maybe I'll stay home."

"That's not a good idea. Come on." She took my arm and we went into my bedroom. My mother tucked me into bed and kissed me good-night.

"Are you in love with Craig?" I asked.

"This is no time to talk about it. We'll talk another time. Go to sleep. I love you."

"I love you, too," I said, and turned over to think. But in minutes I fell asleep.

Chapter Seven

My father didn't wait for Mom to call. Early the next morning, while she was still asleep and I was fixing my breakfast, he phoned. He barely said hello to me before asking to speak to my mother. "If she's there," he added sarcastically.

"Of course she's here," I told him. "But she's still asleep."

"Wake her up." His tone told me not to argue. My stomach turned over uncomfortably. No question there was going to be a fight.

My mom doesn't wake up easily. As a matter of fact, she hates to be woken up, and when she is, it takes her forever to get over the shock because she always thinks something terrible has happened. That morning was no different.

"What is it? What's happened?" She sat up in bed wild-eyed. "Are you all right?"

"Yeah, I'm all right. Dad's on the phone."

"Oh, for God's sake. Tell him I'll call him later." She turned back to her pillow.

"I think you'd better talk to him now. He'll think you're not here."

She opened her eyes wider. "He's got a nerve. Does he think I stayed out all night?"

"No, no, he didn't say that. Mom, he's waiting on the phone. Please."

She gave me another look and groaned. "All right, if you want me to. But he's crazy calling up at this hour of the morning. He doesn't have to check up on me. I don't need that."

I got her robe from the chair and handed it to her. "I hope you don't have a fight."

"If we do it's not my fault," she said grumpily.

Who's fault was it, I thought. Was it my fault for having been born? I remembered running into their room when I was four, five, six years old. It had been delicious to get into bed between the two of them. We used to play games and I felt so safe. I'd close my eyes and say I was thinking of a color, and they had to guess what it was. Or I'd think of an animal. Or sometimes we just rolled around and tickled and hugged each other. It's been only two years, but I'd almost forgotten what it was like to be with the two of them together. It was another world that I would never have again.

They sure were having a fight. My mother was yelling. "I take better care of her than you do. She's almost fifteen years old and perfectly capable of being home alone. Believe me, it doesn't happen every night, and you have a hell of a nerve telling me what to do. I'm not the one who decided to get married and didn't even have the guts to tell her. And out of the blue, presenting her with a stepsister. If she's having problems, and I can tell you she is, it's because of you, not me. When did you last spend some time with her alone? Tell me that."

I didn't want to listen, yet my ears were glued to catching every word. A lot went on back and forth; then my mother said in a calmer tone: "I don't know that I want her to go away to boarding school. But if you want to take her up to New Hampshire to give a look, that's okay. A weekend alone with you would be very good right now. But remember, I'm not making a commitment to sending her away. I'd have to give it a lot of thought and know how she really felt about it."

When she hung up she looked exhausted. "That man wears me out," she said. "He wants to take you up to New Hampshire this weekend to look at a school he thinks is great. But that doesn't mean you have to go—we'll have to discuss it seriously later. But it won't hurt to look at it, and you'll have some time alone with your father. Anyway, it wouldn't be until next year if you should go."

"What else did he say?"

My mother gave me a weak smile. "Plenty. You don't want to hear it. Hadn't you better get going to school?"

"Yeah. What's the name of the school?"

"The Booth School. I never heard of it, but your father seems to think it's terrific."

"What's the matter with Lenox Hill?"

"Would you want to go there?"

"The school's okay, but I wouldn't want to live with Fern. Besides, I'm not sure I want to go away at all."

I had made up my mind to pay attention in school and to concentrate on the work, but it wasn't easy. I managed okay in Mr. Adams's class, but when I got to math it was impossible. My mind kept thinking about my parents' morning fight, going away to school, and wondering about Fern and Paul. I was miles away from the equations Mrs. Jaffe was putting on the blackboard. Mary was no help. She sat next to me and when I leaned over to see what she was writing with such deep concentration, all I could see was a list of boys' names.

"What's that?" I whispered.

Mary held the paper away from her and looked at it dreamily. "These are the boys I've kissed. I hope I didn't forget anyone."

"You kissed all *those?*" There were eight or nine names. "Where?"

Mary giggled. "On the mouth, silly." We both laughed, and of course Mrs. Jaffe rapped her ruler and bawled us out.

As soon as we were out of class, Mary let me look at the paper more carefully. I couldn't believe the boys she'd kissed. "I must be backward," I said. "I've only kissed two boys in my life."

"You'll probably make up for it when you're older," Mary said kindly.

"I may never kiss any boys again." There was no connection except for my general feeling of depression, but I told her about my parents' fight and about going up to New Hampshire with my father.

"I hope you don't go away," she said, and I knew she wasn't just saying it to be nice. She meant it and I did, too, when I told her I wouldn't want to leave her.

For the first time since Ellen and Fern had come to Lenox Hill I was looking forward to the weekend. But the week was a long one. My mother had to go into Boston on business and decided to stay overnight because Craig got theater tickets.

"Are you going to stay with him?" I asked her.

"I don't like that question. No, I am not staying with him. I'm staying with Frances Hunter, and I will give you

66

her phone number just in case. You can stay with Mary, can't you?"

"You can stay with Craig if you want. I don't care and I won't tell Dad." We were sitting at the table after dinner. Neither one of us felt like clearing the plates away.

"Amanda, I wish you would stop worrying about my sex life. First of all, I consider it none of your business; and second, I can take care of it myself, if I want to. It just so happens that right now I am not interested in that sort of relationship. What about you? Sex seems to be on your mind a lot."

"Other girls have kissed a lot more boys than I have. I've only kissed two. Do you think I'm backward?"

My mom shook her head with amazement and laughed. "Is that what's bothering you? I don't really think you have to worry. Two's pretty good for your age. The other girls sound promiscuous."

I asked her what that meant and she said it was being indiscriminate. "If a girl or boy goes around kissing everyone, he or she is promiscuous. It's not nice."

I didn't tell my mother that when I said "other girls" I only meant Mary. Besides Mary was very nice, so the word didn't fit her anyway.

However, when I stayed overnight at Mary's, I tried to explain to her about being promiscuous, and that my mother said kissing a lot of boys wasn't nice.

"I kissed the first boy when I was twelve," she said, "and that's over two years ago, so it isn't so many. Besides, I like it. Do you think I'm going to be wicked when I get older?"

"I hope not." To be honest, I was jealous of her. Not jealous mean, but wishing I wasn't so slow. "I'd like to get experience. Paul and Tubby, who moved away, were the only boys who wanted to kiss me. I guess I'm not the sexy type." There was a bright moon and Mary's curtains were making interesting shadows on the wall. We were in our beds, and her mother had made us turn out our light ages before.

"You're a little standoffish. But that's okay. When a boy really wants to kiss you, he'll let you know. But you have to let him know, too."

"How do you do that? You can't tell a boy that you want him to kiss you."

"No, of course not. But there are ways. You'll find out; it's nothing I can explain."

It was a very unsatisfactory conversation. I wondered if Paul had kissed Fern. I didn't want to think about that so I said good-night to Mary and turned over to go to sleep.

The bus trip on Friday seemed hours longer than usual. At every stop pokey people got off and on. One woman took so long collecting her belongings the bus driver told her he didn't have all day. But at last we got to Lenox Hill.

My father had said he didn't know whether we'd leave for New Hampshire Friday night or early Saturday morning. Of course I was hoping it would be Friday.

When I got to the house, the door was unlocked, but after I called hello as loudly as I could several times, I had to conclude no one was home. I looked around the kitchen. It was very neat except, surprisingly, for a few dishes in the sink. There was no note there, nor on the hall table. I went up to my room—nothing there, either. I went back downstairs and proceeded to get angry.

The living room had Ellen's new rug, an orangey red fringed one made of heavy wool. She had put pillows to match on the sofa, and a large bowl of dark orange flowers on a low table. No newspapers in sight—all the tables clear except for three slim books on one and a small clay figure on another. The room looked like a picture in a magazine, and I got angrier by the minute looking at it. I had a crazy desire to mess it up, to make my presence known, and to destroy the lifeless serenity of that room. I walked up and down furiously: Where were they; why hadn't my father left a note? He knew what bus I took, what time I would get there. I had come so full of excitement, looking forward to the trip with him, hoping he would surprise me and be all ready to take off—the letdown was too much.

I went up to my room and stretched out on my back on the bed. It's a habit I have when I want to think or am depressed. But I was too angry and hurt and restless to stay put. I got up to look out the window to see if anyone was coming. I could see kids from the school walking, but the tennis courts were empty.

When I heard the front door slam, I ran down. My father looked startled to see me. "Oh, Amanda. . . ."

"Sorry if I scared you. I've been here for ages. Where is everyone? Are we going now?"

"Going? Oh, Lord, your trip . . . everything's been driven out of my mind. It's been such a day. Fern's in the hospital. She's okay, just shook up a lot. She banged up my car—totaled it, in fact. Just a few bruises . . . I think I need a drink." I followed my father into the kitchen where he brought out a bottle of brandy and poured himself a small shot.

"You mean we're not going?" I couldn't absorb all he was telling me.

My father looked at me as if I'd gone crazy. "Of course we're not going. Didn't you hear what I said? Fern is in the hospital. The doctor wants her to stay in overnight to make sure she's all right, no concussion or anything. I haven't even got a car—it's smashed up—but I wouldn't go away. I borrowed a school car to come home to get a few things for

Fern. She's only in for one night but she wants her own nightgown and toilet articles and her diary . . . I've got a list here. You can help me get her things together and come back to the hospital with me." My father was fishing through his pockets for Fern's list.

"I don't want to go to the hospital. If there's nothing the matter with Fern, couldn't you borrow the school car and we could go tomorrow morning? She'd be here with her mother."

My father had found a crumpled piece of paper and was studying it. He looked up at me as if he'd only half heard what I said. But he fooled me. "Amanda," he said sharply. "There's been an accident, a bad accident. I'm shook up, Ellen is shook up, Fern narrowly escaped getting killed, and you talk about going away. Can't you think of anyone but yourself?"

"I only thought as long as Fern was all right . . . you don't know how I counted on this weekend. I've been thinking of nothing else all week. I came here, not a soul, not even a note. What was Fern doing with your car anyway—she's not old enough to have a license." I felt close to tears.

"I know that. Thank God another car wasn't involved, that she didn't injure someone else. She ran into a stone wall. Of course she had no business taking my car. It was a very foolish thing to do, but that's past history now."

"Aren't you going to punish her? Are you letting it go, just like that?" My father had gone back to looking at his list for Fern.

"I think she's been punished enough." Then he looked up at me. "What's the matter with you, Amanda? What have you got against Fern?"

"She's adorable," I said, but I don't think my father was listening.

I went up to Fern's room with my father and we got her things together: her nightgown, robe, slippers, brush and toothbrush, a silver pen and her leather-bound diary, plus a book she'd asked for. All the while I was thinking, Why am I doing this; but out loud, I only said, "All this for overnight? That girl is cuckoo."

Even my father looked a little annoyed. "I suppose it will make her feel better. We have to stop on the way back for ice cream. She wants some coffee ice cream."

I gave my father a look, but I didn't say anything until we were downstairs getting into the school station wagon. "If I'd smashed up your car, I bet you wouldn't be bringing me ice cream," I said, sliding into the front seat beside him.

"Probably not. You'd better not try it, if and when I get another car." He had a grim look.

"How come Fern's being treated like she did something great?"

"She's not. However, she and I are trying to establish a relationship, and to me that is the most important thing. Scolding or punishing her now isn't going to accomplish anything. I think she's learned a lesson."

It didn't sound right to me. Because I was his daughter I'd be punished, but because she was someone new she was being handled with kid gloves. Unfair!

I had to admit that Fern looked pretty sick propped up against her pillows in the hospital bed. She gave me a weak smile when we came in, but then lost my sympathy completely when she turned to my father and, before even a thank you, said, "I forgot to ask you to bring the little fuzzy white lamb on my bureau, my mascot. You didn't remember it by any chance, did you?"

"I'm afraid not," my father apologized. "Maybe when we come back tonight I can bring it."

"I thought we'd just stay on," Ellen said. She was sitting

close to the bed, stroking Fern's hand. "We can have a bite in the cafeteria. Visiting hours aren't over until nine. I'd feel better being here."

"Sure, if that's what you want to do," my father said agreeably.

I was still mulling over Fern asking for her little white lamb when she asked for a glass of water, then to have her pillows adjusted, the shade lowered a little, please, and the compress on her forehead changed. She was milking it for all it was worth, adoring being the center of attention. I decided I'd better get out before I either got hysterical watching Dad and Ellen fall over each other to comply, or simply took the little basket of flowers and threw it.

I did neither, but after hanging around for a few more minutes I said I'd go home and get my homework out of the way.

"And how do you plan to get there?" my father asked. "I'm not going to drive you back now. I thought you'd stay here with us."

"I can hitch a ride. Someone's bound to be going to the village and I can walk from there."

My father fussed about my accepting a ride, but I promised I'd wait downstairs and only take a ride with a woman leaving the hospital.

I didn't have to wait long. Soon a very pregnant young woman and her mother came out the front entrance, where I was waiting. I figured I'd be safe with them. They dropped me in front of the drugstore in the village. A group from the school was standing there, and a Lenox Hill van was at the curb. Miss Haley, the drama coach, was walking by, and since she was a friend of my father's I asked her where they were going. She told me to a rock concert over in Springfield. One of the boys said that a fantastic group, the White

Lightnings, was playing. "You want to come?" he asked me.

"Oh, I couldn't. I don't go to the school. My father's a master, but I only come here on weekends."

He asked me who my father was, and when I told him, his face lit up. "Gee, I didn't know he had a daughter. He's a terrific coach. I play soccer with him. Come on, a few kids couldn't make it so there are a couple of extra seats. If your father's in the school, it's okay. No one will know the difference anyway."

The boy who spoke to me wasn't good-looking like Paul—his neck was too skinny, and his forehead took up a lot of his face. But he wasn't bad. He had a friendly smile and looked scrubbed and bright. His voice was deep and low.

I stood there hesitating. "I'd have to go home and leave a note. When do you think we'd get back?" By now Miss Haley was down the block. I had thought that perhaps I could give her a message for my father, but that seemed too complicated.

"I don't know," the boy said. "Maybe late, maybe not. But we're leaving right now, so you wouldn't have time to go home. Come on. Your father's a good sport, and it's not as if you were going anywhere with strangers."

I didn't need a lot more coaxing. Kids were getting into the van, and the boy, Gerry, took me by the arm. We were almost the last to get on. Gerry made for a seat in the back, and we squeezed in together. If I had wanted to change my mind it was too late. The driver started the engine and the van took off.

Chapter Eight

Much to my embarrassment, Gerry spread the word that I was Mr. Maynard's daughter. I then heard a few things about my father: He was popular as a coach and strict in the classroom; no one knew he'd been married before and had a daughter; when he got angry he turned white and speechless (I could have told them that); and when he was wearing a pink shirt it meant he was in a good mood (I knew that, too). One of the girls, Patti, wanted to know if my mother was like Fern's mother. She had gone over to do her homework with Fern, and Ellen hadn't let them play any records. She told them they wouldn't be able to concentrate.

"My mother's nothing like that," I told her. "She doesn't care how I do my homework as long as I get it done."

As we rode, Gerry told me a little about the other kids on the bus and about himself. "Most of the kids in this school have divorced parents," he said. "That's why they're here." Gerry was no exception, but he was cheerful about it. "I don't mind. I like it here. It's better than when I was home and my parents weren't speaking to each other. They were really funny. My mother would give me messages for my father, and he'd give me notes to take to her. Now at least they talk to each other on the telephone."

I liked being with these kids. They weren't at all snobby, and they made me feel that I wasn't alone. Some of them were much worse off than I was. Even though my parents were divorced they still loved and cared about me, and didn't ship me off to boarding school just to get me out of the house.

The concert was in a big hall, and there seemed to be millions of people swarming all over the place. I'd never been to a big star concert before. I could feel electricity in the air, and expectation, as if every girl and boy there was personally bent on connecting with the stars. There was a lot of pushing and shoving, but it was good-natured; no one got rowdy or mean.

I hung on to Gerry and he hung on to me. The kids from Lenox Hill had two rows reserved, but there was a mad scramble for who should sit where and next to whom. Gerry and I got seats next to each other on the aisle.

The hall was noisy and I was afraid it would go on during the concert. But after a tremendous amount of clapping and screaming when the group appeared, everyone quieted down as soon as they began to play.

It was impossible to sit still to that music. You could feel the entire hall of people sway and tap their feet to the wild rhythm from the stage. The feeling was tremendous, like nothing else in the world. Gerry had hold of my hand and we were moving our arms together as if we had been rehearsing for days. Here I was next to a boy I'd only known for about an hour, and I felt that we understood each other perfectly without needing to speak a word.

None of us wanted the music to stop. At the end of the last set, the audience wouldn't let them go. The fans yelled and screamed for more. The poor guys looked exhausted, but they played a couple more songs, and then finally left the stage.

The music had wound everyone up, and the mood of the crowd was different going out. It was a little scary, as if anything could happen—one kid could start something and there'd be a riot in a minute. I'm not crazy about cops, but I was relieved to see a few outside trying to keep everyone in some kind of order as they got on the buses and vans lined up along the street. I was glad when Gerry and I were in our van, in the same backseats we'd had on the ride out.

Then I began to worry about going home. I should have run after Miss Haley and given her a message; I should have gone home and left a note; I should have called home during intermission; I shouldn't have gone to the concert in the first place. The closer we got to Lenox Hill the more nervous I became.

Gerry was talking to me but I wasn't listening. "What's the matter with you?" he asked finally. "You haven't heard a word I said."

"I'm worried about going home. My father will be having a fit."

"What do you think he'll do?"

"I don't know. I've never done anything like this before. Maybe he'll lock me up in my room." I imagined a princess in a tower waiting for a frog to jump into her room and turn into a handsome prince. But with my luck the frog would stay a frog.

"Has he ever done that, lock you up?" Gerry was wide-eyed.

"Hundreds of times." When I realized that he thought I was serious, I told him that no, my father never had. "But maybe he will this time," I added.

By the time the van arrived at the school I was a nervous

wreck. I thought of not going home at all, but where would I go? It was a chilly night and I'd freeze if I slept outdoors.

"What are you going to do?" Gerry asked when we got out of the van.

"What can I do? Go home, I guess."

"I wish I could go with you, but I've got to go straight to the dorm."

"I know. Go ahead, I'll be okay."

"Are you going to be around tomorrow?" he asked.

"I guess so. I usually leave on Sunday."

"Good. I'll see you." He gave me a certain look that made me think if we'd been alone he would have kissed me. I wouldn't have minded.

The kids were all ambling across the green to the dorms, while I dragged my feet up the hill. As each step brought me closer to the house, the more I dreaded reaching it. My father's temper was really something. I remembered the time a few years ago when he came in and found the can of worms I'd left on the kitchen table. I'd needed them for school the next day. He has a thing about worms, hates them worse than snakes. He got hysterical. He thought I'd done it just to upset him and wouldn't believe that I'd simply forgot to bring them up to my room.

He'd yelled, saying he couldn't understand how he'd fathered such a daughter, and ended up feeling sorry for himself. But he couldn't get any sympathy from my mother. She said it was his problem that he couldn't stand worms and not to take it out on me, let alone give me his neurosis.

The trouble with having a fight with my dad is that even when it's over it's not over. I'm afraid to go near him for days while he is quiet and polite, almost apologetic with me. My mom says it's because he feels guilty, but it makes me feel terrible. We usually had such good times together; I hated when we were on the outs.

77

Tonight was worse than the worms. I didn't have a good excuse except that there wasn't time to leave a note. But I knew he'd say I was selfish and mean, only thinking of myself by going when Fern was in the hospital, and I was inconsiderate because I was giving him another worry. I could hear it all before I stepped inside the door.

The house was dark and quiet. For a few minutes I thought, What do you know, they're not even home. Then I saw a light coming from under the door of the living room and I went in. My father was sprawled in his big leather chair with a book in his lap, sound asleep. For a few seconds I thought I could slip upstairs and get into bed without his hearing me, but it didn't work. He opened his eyes and saw me. "Hello," he said sleepily. "What time is it?"

"Almost twelve o'clock." I read the clock on the mantel.

"I've been sleeping for over an hour." He sat up and ran his fingers through his hair. "I'm exhausted. Did you have a good time?"

I couldn't believe my ears. "Yes. Do you know where I was?"

"Yeah. Meg Haley told me, and a good thing, too. You shouldn't have gone without leaving a note," he said mildly. "I've told you a million times not to go off without letting me know where you are." He yawned elaborately. "I'm beat. Ellen stayed over with Fern. I hope that kid's going to be all right. Sometimes a concussion can show up days later. Give her a break when she comes home, Mandy. She didn't need this on top of everything else."

On top of what else? A terrific school, a room all fixed up for her, her mother and my father knocking themselves out for her. . . . I was beginning to boil. He probably didn't care where I was. If I hadn't come home at all he wouldn't have worried. I was a stupid idiot to have thought for a minute he was going to be angry because he'd been worried. He'd been asleep or worrying about his precious Fern all the time I'd been nervous about what he was going to do to me. Amanda Maynard was finished. She was past history, someone to be dumped. My father had a new life now, and I had to face that fact.

I stood in front of him feeling stupid and mean, wanting to do something drastic to make him care, wanting to cry, wanting to run home to my mother. It was the worst moment of my entire life. I'd lost him. If he had died I couldn't have lost him any more than I did as I watched him now bend and pick up the book that had slid off his lap and fallen on the floor. He didn't care about me at all. I hated him.

Up in my room I felt worn out. I couldn't remember ever feeling so tired. I didn't want to think; I didn't want to do anything, not even brush my teeth. I just wanted to crawl into bed.

The next morning when I came downstairs my father was dressed and ready to leave. As far as he was concerned, nothing had happened between us. He didn't know that everything had changed, that I was no longer "his little girl." And I would never let him know that I could never love him the same way anymore.

"I'm going over to get Fern and Ellen," he said in a rush. "Ellen called to say Fern was being discharged early. Do you want to come?" That last sentence was an afterthought.

"No, I haven't had my breakfast. I thought we would have breakfast together."

My father turned back, frowning. "That would have been nice if you'd gotten up earlier."

"You could have woken me. I would have made you eggs

for a change. I make wonderful scrambled eggs with oregano."

"That's your mother's way. I like mine plain."

What was the sense in trying to be nice? He was finished with my mother and with me. I wondered what I was doing there. Just because my parents had made an agreement didn't mean I had to be part of it. Two years ago they hadn't asked me what I wanted to do. They had told me that this was the way it was going to be—the school week with my mom and weekends with my dad. I'd been too dumb to say anything then; besides, how could I have known it was going to turn out to be like this?

Standing there, my father looked like a stuffed pigeon, a little too plump for his old corduroy jacket. Why did I ever think he was good-looking? His face was worn and tired, and I wanted him to put his arms around me and call me his little girl. The truth was I loved him so much I couldn't possibly hate him even if he didn't love me anymore.

"Please don't wander off anywhere," he said. "I want you to be here when we come back." He'd read my mind because that was precisely what I'd thought of doing.

"I'll be here, don't worry."

When they brought the princess home, they fussed and waited on her enough to turn my stomach. If she was sick, or actually hurt, I could understand it, but there wasn't a darn thing the matter with her. Besides, she had taken the car without permission, she had driven it without a license, and she had smashed it up.

On top of everything, Paul came to see her with a bunch of flowers. He said hello to me as if he had never kissed me, and then waved me off like I was some kid he'd seen around. I suppose a kiss meant nothing to him. But I was stupid enough to feel hurt when I watched his face light up

80

as he went over to Fern stretched out on the living room sofa. She played her invalid role to the hilt, smiling weakly at him as he gave her the flowers. I was the dope who got water for them, asked Paul if he wanted something to drink, and then brought in a tray with sodas and cookies for the two of them.

The day had turned soggy and warm for October, more like August thunderstorm weather. Sure enough we heard thunder rolling toward us. The sky got very dark and Ellen was sure a tornado was coming. My father assured her that we didn't have tornados in New England, but she said she'd read about one in Connecticut a couple of years ago. The sky was like night, and suddenly there was a tremendous clap of thunder and all our lights went out. My father was on the porch when it happened, and we could hear him swearing like crazy. With his usual quick temper, he began cursing the utility company, shouting that they should have put their lines underground and that all they cared about was making money—they didn't give a hang for the consumer.

He was mad as heck. He'd gotten out his chain saw and meant to cut up some logs for the fireplace. Ellen tried to calm him down, but I could have told her she was wasting her time. My mother had known better and used to let him alone when he got that way. Actually, she thought he was funny, getting into a hysterical anger over things like flat tires, blown fuses, or stolen wallets. Mom would sit back and keep quiet until he'd yelled himself out. Then he would look sheepish and pretend that he was busy doing something else.

But Ellen was different; she got involved. "Darling, you'll upset your stomach getting so excited. We don't need logs now, we still have enough for a couple of fires. Oh, my. . . ." She held her hands over her ears at another tremendous clap of thunder and shut her eyes against the flash of lightning. Then she took up where she'd left off, following him around, trying to pacify him.

I felt sorry for her. Reasoning with my father was a waste of time. He liked getting mad. Even Fern said, "Mom, why don't you forget it?"

Suddenly my father did a turnabout. Paying no attention to what Ellen said, he put his arms around her and spoke soothingly. "You mustn't be afraid of the storm. We have lightning rods and this house has stood for a long time and will continue to stand." She snuggled up against him, and I could see how he liked to cuddle her slightly plump, soft roundness in a way my mother would never have permitted. I guess Ellen made him feel the big macho man, and I had the feeling that half the time he didn't listen to her chatter. I felt peculiar watching them hold each other.

I had never thought about my father as being sexy until recently; but once I did, it opened up all kinds of thoughts that were upsetting. I wondered if my mother was sexy, too. If she wasn't, could that be why their marriage had broken up? I didn't like thinking about these things because the whole business was a mystery to me. It was hard for me to imagine what actually went on between two people when it came to sex. I wished I could talk to my parents, but I felt awkward asking, and I wasn't sure they'd tell me any more than the facts, which I already knew. I didn't need to be told how babies were born; the things I wanted to know about were less tangible—I wanted to find out about feelings and how it really happened. Yet I realized I would probably have to wait until I was older and learn for myself.

So there I was with Paul hovering around Fern, and my dad and Ellen clutching each other. I felt alone and miserable.

Things didn't improve when the storm subsided and the

sun came out. Some kids from the school came over and Fern was a heroine.

"I saw the car," one of the boys said. "Boy, you really smashed it. That car is *gone*." He said it as if Fern had just won an Olympic championship. He shook his head in disbelief and was joined by some of the others. "She didn't even have a license. Wow."

Those kids were desperate for excitement, a bunch of jerks who thought smashing up my father's car was one big, marvelous act. Gerry came over a little later and that made me feel better. He sat down next to me and I could tell by the way he shook his head that he was thinking the same thing I was. I said to him, "I suppose if she'd killed a few people they'd think that was great, too."

"Super. What do you expect from a bunch of morons?"

"How can you stand living with kids like these?" I asked.

"I can't. But they're not all this bad. I've got a few friends. You going to be here next weekend?"

"Sure."

"Good, we'll do something. I don't know what, but I'll figure something out."

Sitting next to him was nice, apart from the other kids hanging around Fern. We didn't have to talk to understand each other. I liked that.

Chapter Nine

Someone should start a march for teenager's rights. I am sick of having grown-ups make all the decisions about my life. Don't they know that I'm a person—that sometimes *I* like to make the arrangements for where *I'm* to be and what *I'm* going to do. Oh, no, they just tell me, You're to be at your father's house, or you're to be at your mother's house, or you're to visit your grandmother, or stay overnight with your friend Mary. . . . It doesn't seem to occur to anyone that maybe I have some plans of my own.

I was boiling mad. On Wednesday my mother announced that she had spoken to my father and arranged to have Fern come to spend the weekend with me. It seemed that my father and Ellen decided they needed to have a couple of days by themselves and so they were going off on a little trip. This coming weekend.

"But I have a date up at Lenox Hill," I told my mother. "I told Gerry I'd be there and he said we'd do something together. I've been looking forward to it all week." I was ready to scream.

"Gerry will be there another weekend," my mother said calmly. "Don't get frantic."

"I don't know if he'll be there or not. Maybe he'll never ask me again. Why can't they go another weekend? Why does it have to be this one?"

"I don't know, but they decided to go. There's nothing I can do about it."

"Nobody asks me anything," I yelled. "Nobody cares what happens to me. I have a date with a boy I really like and I can't keep it. I don't even know how to call him at school to tell him I won't be there. He'll probably never speak to me again."

"Amanda, it's not the end of the world," my mother said. "You can ask your father to give him a message. I had to change my plans, too. What do you think Fern would like to do when she comes here?"

"I don't know and I don't care. You two can do what you like. I don't even want to see her."

I did everything I possibly could to delay going home on Friday afternoon. I straightened out my desk, cleaned up my locker, and spent some time in the library. When there was absolutely nothing left I could think of, I walked home.

Fern was already there when I arrived. She'd dumped her dirty old duffle on my bed and was sprawled on the sofa with my mother, a bag of potato chips between them, watching TV. My mother didn't even ask why I was home so late. I sat down on a chair and watched the show with them. Very boring. I thought about Gerry. He hadn't looked so skinny last Saturday when I'd seen him at my father's. I liked his eyes and I'd felt he wasn't an ordinary boy. Paul was handsome and made a lot of wisecracks, like someone who wanted people to notice him. Gerry wasn't like that. He was quieter, and when he said something he spoke in a low voice as if he wanted only me to hear him. He had made me feel that even with a lot of people around we were alone. With him I felt special and important. I wondered if he would have been there to meet me at the bus stop since he knew what bus I took.

Fern said that she wanted something to drink and startled me out of my pleasant daydream. Darn her. I could have been with Gerry right now if she wasn't visiting me. While I knew it wasn't her fault that she was there, I couldn't help resenting her—first she steals Paul away, and now she's interfering with Gerry and me.

"Would you like to go out and get a soda?" my mother asked.

"We have some sodas here," I said.

"I thought it might be fun to go out. We could show Fern around the neighborhood." Here we go again, I thought. Now my mother's getting into the act of "Let's be nice to Fern."

So off we went to get a soda. Real exciting. We walked around the neighborhood, but streets of garages, tailor shops, beauty parlors and hardware, electrical supplies, candy, and soda stores weren't that interesting. Fern was attracted to the little candy store where kids from the block hung out. "I bet that's where they go to buy dope," she said.

My mother laughed at her. "Not old Mrs. Greenberg. She'd faint if anyone tried to sell dope in her store. You've got the wrong place."

"You'd be surprised," Fern said darkly. "You can't tell about people these days. In New York you can buy stuff on almost any street corner. Whenever I see bunches of kids hanging around I cross the street."

"I know you should be careful, but I think that's a bit of an exaggeration," my mother replied, then went on to talk about something else. But I noticed that when we did pass any group of people, Fern made a wide circle around them. That girl was weird. One minute she was the nose-up-in-the-air sophisticate, and the next she seemed scared of her shadow. I couldn't figure her out.

My mom had to go out to see a client that afternoon, so when we came home Fern and I listened to records and then played one of my board games while Mom got ready. I still didn't know how to talk to her or what she was interested in. She still gave me the feeling that she had deep secrets she didn't want to talk about with me but that were on her mind.

Every time she lost on the board she had a fit and tried to say that the dice hadn't rolled properly and she should have another chance.

"What difference does it make?" I asked her once. "This game doesn't need brains—if you lose, so what?"

"I don't like losing," she said.

"Who does?"

"I'm not used to losing. When I played games with my father, he always let me win. I know that sometimes I shouldn't have, but it was nice of him to do it."

This was the first time she'd ever mentioned her father and it made me wonder what he was like. It must be peculiar for her to have my dad as a father now. He'd never do anything like that. When you played any kind of game with him, he fought like crazy to win, and he'd never let you cheat or get a point unfairly. Even when I was little and I played checkers with him, I lost all the time. Once my mom asked him to give me a break, but he said if I took my time and used my head I'd win, but I had to do it on my own.

By this time my mother was dressed and ready to leave. She was carrying her large portfolio and looked stunning in a black wool suit. Fern was eyeing her admiringly. "I don't know how long it will be," she said. "We have to go over a bunch of designs. I may be late, so here. . . ." She put down her portfolio and rummaged through her bag until she pulled out a twenty-dollar bill and handed it to me. "If you girls get hungry you can go over to Joe's and get a pizza. When I get back I'll fix a salad and some dessert, but this will hold you for a while. Sorry," she said to Fern, "but business comes first. Tomorrow night we'll have a real dinner."

"I don't mind. I like pizza." She gave my mother a real smile.

I wasn't surprised, after my mom left, to hear Fern say, "Your mother's nice. I like her." That's all she said but there was a look on her face that made me feel sorry for her again. That seemed to be my main feeling about Fern, but it was weird feeling sorry for someone who kept such a wall around herself. Actually, I never knew where I was with her—I never felt at ease the way I was with other girls.

Fern and I hung around for a while and then decided that we were hungry. Even on a pizza we couldn't agree. She wanted just a plain cheese one, and I wanted one with everything on it. We stood arguing until she grudgingly agreed to accept sausage. She suggested taking the pizza home. "So we don't have to buy sodas. You have loads at home," she said. I was surprised that she wanted to save my mother's money.

But I should have known better. The pizza was $4.25, and when we left the shop Fern asked me what I was going to do with the rest of the money. "Give it back to my mom. What else?"

"We could buy some other things," she said. "Or we could divide up the money."

I was carrying the box with the pizza and almost dropped it. "You mean *keep* it?" I was truly shocked. "What makes

88

you think my mother wouldn't ask for it?" I couldn't imagine what went on in that girl's head.

"You could just say you spent it. She wouldn't care . . . she doesn't ask a lot of questions." Usually I walk quickly, but I had to slow down to stay with Fern. She wasn't in a hurry to get home.

"In the first place, you don't know my mother. But even so, I wouldn't do anything like that. That's like stealing." I looked her straight in the eye. She looked back at me, but at least her face clouded over. "So what?" she said. "It's your mother, so the money is probably partly yours anyway. I bet she gets money from your father to take care of you. Do you get any of it?"

"Not directly. I get an allowance. But Mom pays for my clothes and food, and the rent and stuff. I don't need any other money."

"Whether you need it or not, you're not getting it. So the twenty dollars your mother gave you is as much yours as hers."

I shook my head. "I don't think so. She earns money, too. I think she spends all that my dad gives her on me, maybe more. Anyway, I'm not keeping this money, so forget it."

Fern didn't seem the least bit put out by our conversation, but believe me, it bothered me. I'd never known anyone like Fern, and I couldn't figure her out. There was plenty of stealing in our school, but most of us knew who did it. And the few who did it weren't the kind of kids I'd have for my friends. Yet now I had Fern, who was part of my family. It made me feel strange.

When we got home, I began to worry about some money I had in my bureau drawer. I had this awful picture of Fern sneaking into my room when I was busy someplace else and going through my drawers to see what I had. It was a terrible feeling to be living with someone who stole. She was cool about it, too, as if it was perfectly okay. She made me feel there was something wrong with *me* because I wouldn't have any part of it. I'm certainly no goody-goody, and I don't want anyone to think I am, but I'm not a thief.

It was one weird weekend. Fern was watching when I gave the money back to my mother. She shook her head and rolled her eyes behind my mother's back, as if to say that I was being a dope. The whole time I was a nervous wreck for fear she'd take something of my mother's. Saturday morning, after breakfast, my mother couldn't find her opal ring. My heart sank. She said she'd taken it off when she washed the breakfast dishes and left it on the counter, but it wasn't there. I was afraid to look at Fern for fear I'd know by her expression that she'd taken it. We looked all over the kitchen, and oddly enough it was Fern who found where it had rolled on the floor under a cabinet. My mother was delighted and thanked her profusely. Yet I had a funny feeling that the ring hadn't been on the floor at all, but that Fern had had it and decided to give it back.

It was a terrible way to think, to be so suspicious of someone living with you. I hated myself for not believing Fern, although I knew I had good reason not to trust her.

I dreaded being alone with her. I didn't know how to talk to her; besides, this stealing business made being natural impossible. Saturday afternoon I asked Mary and Freddie to come over. Fern cheered up the minute there was a boy around. She turned into a different person. Instead of looking as if she was carrying some heavy weight around, she smiled, laughed, and talked about some of the things she and her friends did in New York. She made me feel foolish, because I had been telling Mary and Freddie what a drag she was, and here she was being so attractive. They would think I had been jealous and mean.

* * *

Just one more day to get through, I thought when I woke up on Sunday morning. It was almost ten o'clock and Fern was taking a three o'clock bus. Five hours and the visit would be over. I was in no hurry to get up and I lay in bed listening to my mother and Fern in the kitchen. When I did get up I found them having breakfast. I got myself a bowl of cereal and joined them. Like the rest of the small apartment, the kitchen looked shabby compared to my father's house.

Fern's eyes wandered from the paint peeling on a wall to the scarred cabinets. "My mother and I lived in a place like this," she remarked. "After my father died we moved out of our big house. My mother wanted to be in the city."

"I thought you'd always lived in New York," I said.

"No, we had a house out on Long Island. Near a beach. It was great in the summertime."

"You probably missed it when you moved to the city." My mother was pouring coffee and didn't see Fern's eyes turn away. It looked like she was fighting back tears.

"I sure did. I missed the school the most; I hated having to change."

"Me, too, when we moved here." Our eyes met, and suddenly I felt an unexpected bond of sympathy between us.

But as usual, it didn't last. Fern's next sentence once again pushed me away. "By the way, some boy named Gerry asked me when you were coming up this weekend. I told him you weren't. He wanted to know where he could call you, but I didn't know your phone number, so I told him I didn't know. I think he wanted to talk some more but I was in a hurry to get to class. He looked like kind of a drip anyway."

I thought I'd explode. "Thanks a lot. Why'd you wait so long to tell me? I might have wanted to call him. He's not a drip; he's a lot smarter than your friend Paul Rickenbacker."

"Paul's no brain," Fern said good-naturedly. "But he's awfully good-looking. Sorry about Gerry, I just forgot. Do you like him?"

I didn't want to answer. I mumbled, "Maybe. I don't know." I sure had no desire to confide in Fern.

I wasn't sorry to see her go. When my mother and I walked back from the bus stop, Mom said, "That girl has a lot of problems. I don't think she's happy."

"Why not? She's got everything. She's pretty, she lives with her mother and a father, she doesn't have to move from one place to another every week, she's going to a great school. I don't see what she has to complain about."

"None of it means she doesn't have problems. Losing her own father, moving to a new town, going to a new school, having a new stepfather can't all be easy. You don't know what she may be going through."

"You're not going to get me to feel sorry for her," I said. I wondered what my mother would think if she knew Fern had wanted to keep her money.

It was a drizzly day and when we got home I felt tired and cranky. I kept thinking about Gerry and feeling furious with Fern for not telling me sooner that he'd asked about me. And she could have tried to give him my phone number— all she had to do was ask my father for it.

I was in my room feeling aimless when my mother came in and asked if I'd seen the ten-dollar bill she'd left under a pitcher in the kitchen. My heart sank.

"No, I didn't see it. You sure you left it there?"

"Of course I'm sure. I put it there this morning to remind myself to pay Mrs. Greenberg tomorrow for the newspapers. I like to pay her every Monday morning, and I didn't want to forget."

Although I went into the kitchen with her and we searched all over, I knew it was a waste of time.

"This is ridiculous," my mom said. "It was here this morning. It's got to be here."

"It's not here," I said. "I know where it is."

My mother looked at me aghast. "You know where it is and you've let me tear this place apart? What's the matter with you, Amanda? Where is it?"

"Fern has it."

"What in heaven's name are you talking about? How could Fern have it?" My mother was standing in the kitchen with her arms folded, looking as if she was ready for a fight.

"She has it because she took it." I drew a deep breath. "Fern is a thief."

"Amanda Maynard, you are making up a story and it's not nice. I realize that you don't like Fern, and I know you have your reasons. But you have no right to say such a thing. That's just plain mean." My mother glared at me. Five minutes before, when she was down on the floor looking for her ten dollars, she had looked like a kid. Now, all of a sudden, she looked like a mother, stern and full of righteousness.

"I'm not being mean and it's the truth." I then told her about Fern's stealing the silk scarf and her wanting to keep the rest of my mother's twenty dollars. Mom's eyes grew wide as she listened.

"Are you really telling me the truth?" she asked. "You're not making this up?"

I looked her straight in the eye. "Would I make up such a story? Honestly, Mom . . ."

"I know, of course not. I'm sorry. It's just so shocking.

It's hard for it to sink in. Let's look some more. Maybe she didn't take this ten bucks . . . I just can't believe it."

So we searched some more, but finally Mom had to give up. We both sank down on the sofa in the living room, exhausted.

"I'm going to have to tell your father," my mother said.

"No. Please don't. He'll never believe me. Fern'll deny it—it will just make a mess. Please, Mom, promise me you won't tell him."

"But it's not right. Fern must be a terribly disturbed girl. She may need help. Besides, she can get into a lot of trouble. Oh, dear, I'm not sure what I should do. . . ." She lay back against the pillows with a deep sigh. "I wish . . ."

"You wish Dad hadn't gotten married, don't you?" I said in a soft voice.

"Sometimes I do. Only because it's hard on you. Nothing's ever a hundred percent right or wrong . . . marriage, divorce . . . it's always mixed and you have to weigh the good against the bad."

"Are you sorry you got divorced?"

"Of course I am, sometimes. I know it was the best thing to do, yet I'm sorry it had to happen and wish that it hadn't."

"Would you have gotten divorced if I hadn't been born?" Her answer was important to me and I kept looking at her face.

"What a question to ask. You had nothing to do with it. I can't imagine life if you hadn't been born." She leaned over and hugged me. "You're the best thing that ever happened to me."

It was funny the way we both stopped talking about Fern until much later that evening.

Chapter Ten

It was agreed: Mom would not say anything to my father yet. She decided that she'd take some time to think about it, but in the meantime she hoped that I would face Fern frankly and hear what she had to say.

That scared me. How do you go up to someone and say, "Are you a thief?" Of course Fern knew that I knew about the scarf, also that she wanted to keep my mom's money— but I had to ask her if she took the ten dollars. And then what? If she said yes, where would I go from there?

Mom and I talked about it back and forth the whole week until I was sick of thinking about Fern. I didn't need this problem on top of everything else. Nothing was going right. Freddie's cheerful face became boring, my marks were still going down, even Mary was bugging me about them.

On Thursday Mary and I went for a walk after school. It was a crisp, sunny November day, the kind of day that usually made me feel super. But I was getting nervous about facing Fern, and Mary with her eagle eye detected that something was wrong.

When we came back to my house to make cocoa—my mom was out so we had the place to ourselves—Mary made me talk and I spilled the whole story.

"Wow." Mary was dumbfounded. "That's awful. What are you going to do?"

"I wish I knew. I can't believe that a few months ago I was a happy kid. Relatively, anyway. I wasn't crazy about my parents being divorced, but I could live with that. I had to. But now this. It's too much. I don't even know how to act with Ellen anymore, and I feel I'm keeping something back from my father. What should I do?"

"Maybe you should just forget it." Mary held a cup so I could pour out the hot cocoa. We mixed some of my mother's coffee in it so it had a rich mocha flavor, and added lots of sugar. "Act like nothing happened."

"That's what Fern does. My mother wants me to talk to her. I'd like to, but I don't know what to say."

"Ask her why she does it. It seems so dumb. One time she'll get caught."

I brought out some cookies and we sat at the kitchen table looking gloomy. "I don't know what good my talking to her is going to do. She'll think I have a heck of a nerve, and she'll make me promise not to say anything. It won't do a darn thing."

"At least she'll know she's not fooling you, and that your mother knows. Maybe that'll scare her into not doing it anymore."

"Maybe. Or maybe she'll kill me for telling my mother."

"It's your mother's ten dollars that's missing. You had a right to tell her." As usual Mary's practical mind made sense.

I took a later bus to Lenox Hill that Friday because I had wanted to get some of my homework out of the way before the weekend. It was just about time for supper when I got to

96

Dad's house. I stopped at the garage to say hello to him. He was busy doing something at his workbench. He looked okay and gave me a great bear hug.

"How was your week? Getting your schoolwork done?" he asked.

"I did most of my homework before I came. That's why I'm late. How are things with you?" I searched his face for a true answer.

"They're coming along." He looked up from the box of washers he had dumped out on the table and was rummaging through. "It takes time. I think Fern's getting adjusted. She's making friends."

"Are you happy?" I really wanted to know.

My father smiled. "Yes, Mandy, I'm happy." It was hard to know from his face if it was real or just something he said. I wanted to believe it was real. "Ellen is good for me." I wanted to ask him more but he turned back to what he was doing. I felt the familiar chill I'd been getting from him since his marriage, whether they were the vibes he meant to send out to me or not. It was like he'd taken care of me and was anxious to go back to what he was doing. I felt shy about even leaning over to kiss him again. I'm losing him, I thought; and for the first time I felt it was not something I was imagining: He may think he still loves me but he's not *interested* in me anymore. His mind is with them.

Fern and her mother were in the kitchen, and I could tell when I walked in that they had been arguing. Ellen gave me her usual gushy greeting, but Fern was cool. I soon found out what their argument was about. Fern was wearing a new white silk blouse that she'd said was $19.95 and her mother had given her twenty dollars to buy. But Ellen had picked up the price tag from the wastebasket and discovered it was really $29.95. Now she wanted to know where Fern had gotten the extra ten dollars. Fern told her she had been saving some of her own money, but I could have told Ellen where it really came from.

As it turned out, however, what was really bothering Ellen was that Fern spent so much money on a blouse. "You should have asked me first," Ellen said. "Whether it's your money or not doesn't matter. It's too much to spend on a blouse you'll have to dry clean after you wear it, it's too tight, and won't fit you in six months. I don't like you wasting money whether it's yours or mine—and besides, all the money comes from me. You don't have any real money of your own."

"That's not my fault," Fern mumbled. "If you let me have some of the money *my* father left, I wouldn't have to ask you for everything." She spat out the word "my."

Ellen glanced at me, embarrassed. "Your father didn't leave much money, and his insurance policies were made out to me. You're not starving, are you?" She was trying to make light of their talk.

"I darn near was when you went off to Europe and left me with practically nothing." Fern threw me a glance that was daring me to make any comment. She didn't have to worry; I had no desire to say a word.

Things calmed down by the time my father came in, and after supper Ellen and Dad decided to go to a movie. Neither Fern nor I wanted to see it, though, so we stayed home.

I knew that this was my chance to talk to Fern if I was ever going to do it, but I still hadn't figured out how to start or what to say. When Fern said she was going up to her room to read, I thought that was the end of a chance to talk. But I screwed up my courage before she had a chance to leave. "I think that ten dollars you had belonged to my mother," I said. I spoke quietly, not wanting to sound angry or excited.

Fern shot me a startled, swift glance and then composed her face into its usual bland, secretive expression. "Where'd you get that crazy idea? You heard me; it was my own money that I'd saved."

"My mother was missing ten dollars after you left. She'd left it on the kitchen counter and it was gone. We searched every inch of the kitchen, the whole house. I'm sure you took it. My mother is, too." I blurted this last part out fast, but I looked at her, not afraid to look her straight in the eye.

She looked back at me defiantly. "You have one heck of a nerve accusing me of taking your mother's lousy ten dollars. What do I need it for? I've got my own money. Maybe you took it and you're trying to dump it on me. I know you hate me, and I guess this is your way of showing it."

We stood in the kitchen, staring at each other like two boxers in the ring, ready to pounce. She was even jumping around the way a fighter does before he's ready to give the first blow.

"I don't hate you," I said. "I feel sorry for you. I know you steal. Who do you think you're kidding? You even showed me that scarf you took from the store. And I know you wanted to keep the change from my mother's twenty dollars. My mother knows it, too. She wants to talk to my father about your stealing."

"You rat," Fern yelled. "How dare you tell your mother stories about me." She was in a rage now. Her face turned white and tense with fear, and she looked like a different person. Although her eyes blazed, they looked frightened, like a small animal that had been trapped.

We were screaming at each other, and she was trying to get at me to pull my hair when we heard the front door slam and her mother walked in. We stepped away from each other.

"What's going on here?" Ellen demanded, depositing her handbag on the kitchen table.

"What are you doing home?" Fern asked.

"There was a big line and we didn't feel like waiting." Ellen was looking from one of us to the other. Fern's face was now flushed and embarrassed. I felt I was a mess.

"Where's my father?" I asked.

"He's out in the garage. He wanted to finish something he was working on. Will you girls please tell me what's going on? I could hear you screaming even before I came in. What are you fighting about?" Ellen's soft face couldn't actually look stern—it was more anxious and worried than anything else.

Fern tossed her head. "Amanda was accusing me of stealing," she said airily. "The creep."

Ellen turned to me with a shocked face. "Of all things. How could you do such a thing?" She shook her head in disbelief. "This is going to far. I've tried to be nice to you. I've been patient, done everything I can to make you feel this is your home as well as your other one . . . but this is too much. You are a mean, ungrateful child."

"I don't know what you've done for me. You haven't done anything," I yelled. "Besides, it's true. You ask Fern about her silk scarf, ask her again where she got the ten dollars for that blouse she's wearing. Just ask her. Lord knows what else she's taken, but I know about those two. I'm not a liar and I don't make up stories about people."

Ellen looked as if she was about to cry. "I can't cope with this." She threw up her hands in despair. "I love your father but I can't handle you, Amanda. I'm not strong enough— I'm not used to this kind of thing. I don't think our marriage is going to work with you around; it can't."

Fern had a satisfied look on her face. I realized she was enjoying the whole scene—her mother's distress, my anger. She doesn't want the marriage to work, I thought, she wants them to break up . . . she'd be rid of me and my father. It was a whole new thought that sent my head reeling.

"I'm going out," Ellen said in a quieter voice. "I've got to think, and I think best when I'm driving quietly, alone." She kissed Fern. "Don't let that child hurt you. I have a serious decision to make," she added, and walked out of the house. My father's rented car had been left in the driveway and we heard Ellen start it up and drive away.

A few minutes later my father came in from the garage. The strain must have shown on our faces because the first thing he said was, "What's the matter?" Then, before we had a chance to answer, he asked where Ellen was.

"She's gone out," I told him. "She went out for a drive."

He looked astonished. "What on earth for? All alone . . ."

"My mother was very upset," Fern said coldly. "Your daughter has been accusing me of stealing." With that she marched out of the kitchen and up to her room.

My father turned to me. He looked as if Fern's announcement was the last straw he could contend with. He sat down heavily on a kitchen chair. "Now, what is all this about?"

"She's been stealing," I told him. And then I gave him a detailed account of the scarf episode, the pizza money Fern wanted to keep, and the missing ten-dollar bill that matched up with what she spent on her new blouse. My father listened with a patient but pained expression on his face.

When I was finished he gave a deep sigh and said, "It's hard to believe. Are you sure about the scarf? She may have paid for it."

"She didn't. She told me she didn't and that she thought

it was okay because it was overpriced. I'm telling you the truth."

"You don't know about the ten dollars. You're only assuming that—you have no proof."

"I know I haven't, but it couldn't have just disappeared. I might have known you would defend her."

"I'm not defending anyone," my father said wearily. "I just want to be sure you're not exaggerating what she's done because you're unhappy about her being here, or jealous, or whatever."

"You mean you don't believe me. Why don't you come out and say so? You think I'm lying . . . that's fine, my own father. Thanks a lot." I was close to tears. I wanted him to come over to me near the window, put his arms around me, and tell me that he still loved me. I wanted everything to be the way it used to be before he married Ellen and had Fern for a daughter.

"I don't think you're lying," he said, hedging. "But you could be building something up, or making assumptions. I don't believe that Fern is a thief."

"She is," I yelled. "Besides that, she's not a very nice person. She's two-faced and selfish. She doesn't care about anyone but herself."

"I can see that you don't like her," my father said dryly. "I'm sorry about that. I was hoping you two girls would be good friends, would be sisters."

"Never. Never in a million years." My father and I faced each other across an abyss much wider and deeper than the three or four feet of kitchen floor between us.

Then he stood up abruptly. "I'm going out to find Ellen."

"You haven't got a car," I said. "How would you know where to go?"

"I'll get a school car. There are a few places I think she might drive to. The only places she knows."

102

Some weekend, I thought, standing by myself in the empty kitchen. I considered going home to my mother, but she had left for the weekend and the thought of an empty house didn't appeal to me. I wished I knew what dorm Gerry was in—I could find him and at least go out for a walk. I sat down at the table feeling lower than low. No one, I resolved, was going to make me come here every weekend after this. I didn't care what agreement my mother had signed. I hadn't been asked and I didn't have to do what it said.

I was more depressed than I'd ever been, but I felt too mad to cry. I felt miserable, deserted, but furious that my own father didn't believe me and that he'd left me to go look for Ellen. Didn't he know that I was the one who needed him desperately, needed a sign that he still loved me a little?

I was still sitting there moping when Fern came downstairs. She was dressed to go out and was carrying a small suitcase.

"Where are you going?" I asked, not really caring where she went.

"I'm leaving here. I'm going to my grandmother's. I hate this house, and I hate living here."

She took me by surprise, but I suddenly woke up to what was happening.

"You mean you're leaving here for good? To live with your grandmother?"

"I don't know where I'll live, but it sure won't be here."

She walked out of the house. I sat where I was, thinking rapidly: I can't let her do this. I would be the one to get the blame. Everything had gotten out of control, had gone too far—Ellen walking out, my father rushing after her, and now Fern leaving. In a short time, less than an hour, my whole world had gone from bad to worse. Only because I had spoken up and told the truth about Fern. I felt sick with

103

guilt—I should have kept my mouth shut—except I'd had this idea, and so had my mother, that if I leveled with Fern maybe she wouldn't steal anymore. We were both wrong. If the marriage busted up, it would be both our faults. We had both wanted it to happen, thought we wanted it; but if it happened now, this way, there would be only misery for all of us.

I got up and ran out of the house after Fern. I couldn't see her but I headed for the bus stop since that seemed the logical place she would go. I ran down the hill, my hair flying. Running made me feel good—taking some action, doing *something* was better than sitting and thinking.

She was at the bus stop, leaning against a tree, her suitcase on the ground close to her legs. Instead of the curved heels she usually wore, she had on flats, a pair of jeans, and a dark windbreaker. She looked forlorn standing by herself.

Now that I was down the hill I didn't know what to do, whether to let her see me or wait until she got on the bus and then get on after her. I stayed behind some trees so that she couldn't see me, and before I'd made up my mind whether to face her or not, the bus came along. I watched Fern get on, and then a couple of other people who came hurrying down the street. I jumped in at the last minute. While I was buying my ticket, Fern glanced up and our eyes met. She looked very annoyed at seeing me, but I expected that. I ignored the warning signals she was sending and marched down the aisle and took the empty seat beside her.

"What do you think you're doing?" she said to me angrily. "Why are you following me?"

"I needed to talk to you. If you leave it's just going to make everything worse. Then your mother'll go, and their marriage will be busted up. It will be terrible." I was pleading with her.

"I don't care if it is busted. But my mother won't leave because of me. She'll be glad to be rid of me. I've been a nuisance to her ever since my father died." She said it quite matter-of-factly, as if she'd been thinking about it for a long time.

"I thought your mother adored you." I wasn't being sarcastic or funny; I really believed that.

"That's what you think," Fern said with a grim little smile. "Don't believe all her gushy stuff—she doesn't give a hang about me. My father loved me; he was the one who cared about me. My mother went off to Europe last summer, that's where she met your father, and left me with an awful old housekeeper. I hated that woman. My mother could have taken me with her."

"Maybe she didn't have the money," I suggested.

"That's what she said. If she didn't have enough for the two of us she shouldn't have gone. She said she needed to get away—well, so did I. All she thinks about is that she lost her husband. What about me? I lost my father. That can be worse."

Fern turned away and stared out the window. I didn't know what to say. Her face looked miserable, and I felt sorry for her.

After a while I said, "Well, you have a father now."

She turned to me fiercely. "I have *not*. You have a father, my mother has a husband, but I don't have a father." There was so much anger in her voice it took me a few minutes to realize she was not only furious but suffering.

"He's trying to be a father to you. He's paid so much attention to you I've been jealous," I said. I was getting angry. My father was going all out for her and she didn't even know it. What more did she want?

"*You've* been jealous?" she looked at me scornfully. "You've got it all: a terrific mother and a father who adores

105

you, really does, not just putting on a show. He doesn't gush, but I can tell. He's nice to me because he thinks it's his duty. You've got nothing to complain about."

"You think I like having my parents divorced—going back and forth every week from one to the other? You're feeling so sorry for yourself you don't even see that other people have a hard time, too. I think that's why you steal, because you think the world owes you something. You think you're getting back at people." She gave me a swift look that made me think I had hit home.

The bus had been moving all the time we'd been talking, but now it was pulling to a stop at the next town. "Let's get off," I said. "We can go someplace and talk."

"You can get off. I don't know why you got on in the first place. I'm going to my grandmother's." She sat with her arms folded and a set expression on her face.

"Please don't. If we got off and talked, you could still go to your grandmother's. The buses run almost every hour. Please."

"I don't know what you think you're going to accomplish," Fern said.

But I felt that she was weakening. I pleaded quickly, got hold of her suitcase, and started walking away. With a sulky look she followed me. We had a hassle with the bus driver to give us back our money for the unused part of our tickets, but he finally did, grumbling about dumb kids who don't know what they're doing.

It was dark out and the bus stop was in a rundown, deserted area. But there were a few stores, a liquor shop, a newsstand, and a dinky coffee counter. I headed for the coffee shop with Fern following. We sat down at the counter and both ordered Cokes.

"I don't know why I'm here," Fern said. "I was stupid to get off that bus. I can't imagine what made me do it."

"Because you don't really want to go to your grandmother's," I said firmly. I didn't quite know what I was doing there, either, but I was determined to bring Fern home to my father's. Some hunch, or instinct—I wouldn't know what to call it—kept telling me that if she left, the marriage would fall apart, my father would be miserable, and I'd be the one to blame. I wasn't being all that altruistic—I didn't want to be responsible for the consequences of Fern's taking off.

We drank our sodas in silence, Fern looking more downcast by the minute. She still had that scared look in her eyes, and I had the impression that she was falling apart in front of me. I felt older, more secure than she was.

When we finished, she said, "What do we do now?" She sounded like she really wanted me to tell her, that it wasn't just a meaningless question. I had never seen anyone change this way: from being angry and defiant to seeming helpless, like a little kid waiting for her mother to tell her what to do. She made me feel terribly grown-up.

"We'll get the next bus back and go home. I think I should call my father; he's probably worried sick."

I tried to get my father on the phone, but there was no answer. We also learned that we had to wait almost an hour for the next bus back. The woman in the coffee shop said we could wait there, so we sat together over in a corner.

Fern still looked sad and forlorn, but after sitting in silence for several minutes I asked her, "What makes you think your mother doesn't care for you?"

She gave me a startled look. "I just know it. After my father died we could have stayed in our house, taken in boarders. But she wouldn't hear of it, said she couldn't bear to live there without him. I felt just the opposite, like he was still around when we were there. I felt he would have wanted us to stay—he loved that place. We were deserting him when we left."

"But maybe it made her sad," I said. "My mother wanted everything different when she and my dad split. We moved into town."

"But you still had your father," Fern said. "That was different. My mother didn't care about my feelings, just her own."

"I guess she thought you'd get used to your new place." I couldn't hold back a deep sigh. "Parents always think we can adjust to anything they want—when they mess up everything they think we kids can take it, can get along fine." I was getting to feel as morose as she was. It was catching.

"Yeah," Fern said, brightening up. "Grown-ups stink. My father was okay; he wasn't like most old people."

"He wasn't very old, was he?"

Fern shook her head. "No, I didn't mean that he was old. He was pretty young, as a matter of fact. I wish he hadn't died."

"Did you always steal, I mean, before. . . ."

"No." Fern's narrow face was serious. "It started when my mother went to Europe. I got so mad that she was going . . . she'd been yapping so about money and then she goes off on a trip like that. She said it was very inexpensive for that kind of a tour and she'd never have a chance again. I hated being left with that dimwitted old lady. It was a real drag." Fern gave an unexpected giggle. "The first time I took anything it was from her. I was mad because she wouldn't let me go overnight to the beach with my friends, said she wouldn't take the responsibility. A real hot weekend, too. She'd cashed her social security check and I took five dollars from her pocketbook. It was funny, she got so crazy looking for it and trying to remember where she'd spent it. I laughed myself silly watching her figure over and over again every penny she'd spent that day, and always coming out five dollars short."

"It must have been funny," I said, but I didn't think her story was funny—I'd have hated it if anyone did that to me. "Don't you worry about getting caught?"

"Sure. I worry a lot. Actually, it's not fun anymore. I get so nervous and when I take something, like that scarf, I never want to wear it. I'm scared someone'll see it, maybe someone from the store, and they'll know I stole it."

"Why do you do it then? Why don't you stop?"

"I keep thinking I will, but then something happens and I've got to do something crazy, something to show them. That's the only thing I can think of, so I do it."

She looked very unhappy, and I felt sorry for her. I wished my mother were there to talk to her.

I bought a chocolate bar and we divided it in half and sat eating it slowly until the bus came. I was afraid she'd change her mind and not get on it, but she followed me without a word, letting me carry the suitcase as if I were her mother or something. We rode back on the bus in silence. I guessed she was worried about what we'd say when we got there, and so was I.

Chapter Eleven

My father was on the phone when we walked into the house. The minute he saw us he yelled, "They're here," and hung up abruptly. "I was talking to the school security guard. We were thinking of calling the police. . . ." He threw his arms around me. Ellen had been nervously pacing up and down the front hall where the phone was, and I saw her reach out her arms to her daughter. Fern allowed her mother to hug her, but she squirmed away pretty quickly. When my father and I pulled apart, Fern was looking at us with a wistful expression on her face.

My father still had his arm around me as he led us into the living room and we all sat down. He pulled me close to him on the sofa. Fern sat down on the floor and her mother pulled a lounge chair near her and flopped into it.

Dad looked around at the three of us with a sheepish grin. "I'm so glad to see you I can't even be angry. Maybe later I'll warm up to it, but for heaven's sake where were you? What happened?" He stretched his arm out to Ellen and pulled her out of her chair to sit next to him on the sofa. She looked at him lovingly, and took his hand and held it tightly.

Fern watched this scene with an expressionless face and looked to me to answer my father. "Fern was upset," I said. "She was going to spend a few days with her grandmother. I went after her and persuaded her to come back."

"I was going to *live* with my grandmother," Fern corrected me in a soft voice.

"I know Fern was upset," my father said. "So was her mother—we all were. I think you owe us an explanation." He turned to me, trying to look stern. "You made some serious accusations."

I looked him straight in the eye. "I was telling the truth. Ask Fern."

I held his eyes until I looked at Fern, who wouldn't look at me. She was making circles on the rug with her finger, one after another. Finally she looked up. Not at me or her mother, but directly at my father. "She was telling the truth. I stole the scarf. I took her mother's ten dollars—but I'll give it back. I'll save it out of my allowance." Her tone was saying, Don't worry about me; I'll take care of everything. She managed to be both apologetic and defiant.

Her mother was horrified. "You're just saying that, Fern; you can't mean it. You don't have to protect Amanda. You're not a thief. I don't believe it."

"You don't believe anything about me," Fern said angrily. "You don't believe I miss my father, that I felt all alone when you went off to Europe. You don't believe I'm a mess—a thief—and not the most beautiful, smartest, most popular, and special person you want me to be. I'll never be what you want me to be. I'm a failure," she yelled.

Fern got up and ran out of the room. Ellen rose to go after her but my father put out a restraining hand. "You stay here, darling. Let me handle this—that child needs a father

111

right now." He went after Fern. We could hear him race up the stairs after her.

Ellen stood up and started pacing around the room, throwing tear-stained glances at me. "I'm sorry, Amanda; I'm terribly sorry I was unfair to you. I never dreamed Fern could do things like that—she's always been such a lovely girl. She didn't need to be special for me, she just was. Always popular, getting good marks, she never gave us a minute's trouble. Her father adored her—I know his loss was terrible for her—and somehow she's held that against me. I felt that if one of us had to go she wished it had been me, not him." She was talking as if she had to get all this out. I don't think she cared whether I heard her or not.

"I went to Europe partly because I thought it would be good for both of us to get away from each other for a while. I know I needed to get away desperately, see some new faces, and get a new perspective on my life. I joined a tour because I was afraid to go alone, and I thought it would be good for Fern to be on her own, to be away from me. We were both becoming too dependent on each other; it wasn't good for either of us. How could she think I was abandoning her. . . . It's hard to understand. . . ."

She kept walking around, tears wetting her cheeks. She was like a child and I could see why she and my father were attracted to each other—she needed someone to take care of her and my father was good at that. He didn't have that with my mother; she wouldn't let anyone take care of her.

"What are they doing up there?" Ellen looked to me for advice. "Do you think I should go up?"

"No, I think you'd better wait down here. They're probably talking."

"But they're taking so long."

"They'll come down." It was so odd: I felt more comfortable with Ellen than I ever had, as if a wall between us had been knocked down. For the first time I felt that I knew the kind of person she was—not very smart like my mother, but sweet, wanting to do the right thing, not mean. Maybe my mother had been too smart for my father, and he needed someone who looked up to him and leaned on him. Ellen was okay, although I knew I never wanted to be like that—I was glad my own mother was different.

Finally my father came down alone. He put his arms around Ellen and kissed her. "Why don't you go up now. I think Fern would like to see you."

"Is she all right?" Ellen asked anxiously.

"Yes, she's fine."

It was my own father I felt strange with. He sat down beside me on the sofa and stretched out his legs in front of him. "I'm sorry you had to go through all this," he said. "I never wanted you to have any of the burden of my new family . . ." He gave a deep sigh. "I was dumb enough to think it would all go smoothly. Ellen is such a darling, and wants to love you, and Fern, too. . . . I thought the three of you would just naturally fall in together. I should have known it wouldn't be so easy."

"I'm okay. Don't worry about me." We sat silently for a few minutes.

"This has been quite a night. Don't ever do that, Mandy. Don't go off and not leave a note, some word where you are. We were worried sick. I suppose your mother would think you should be punished. . . ."

"No, she wouldn't," I said quickly. There was so much I wanted to say to him, but as he said, it wasn't easy. Yet if I kept quiet he would never know. "I didn't think you'd worry about me." I spoke in a low voice. "I didn't think you cared."

"How can you say such a thing?" Dad sounded really upset. "You can't really believe that."

"But I do believe it. I have been thinking it. That night when I came home late from the concert, I was afraid you'd be worried. You didn't sound like you cared at all. You seem always to be concerned about Fern. I didn't count anymore."

My father covered his face with his hands and didn't say anything for a minute. When he lifted his head his eyes were sad. "It's awful how people misunderstand each other. I love you, Amanda, maybe more than anyone else in the world. I knew where you were that night—I told you I'd gotten a message from Meg Haley. And yes, I've tried hard to reach out to Fern; she's a troubled girl. I think you know that. I guess I felt so secure about you and me that I took our relationship for granted. It never occurred to me that you needed to be told that I love you. You're so mature in so many ways I guess I forget how young you are. I thought you'd understand about Fern so easily. . . ." He reached out and put his arms around me. "I'm sorry. And never think that you don't count with me. You always will; no one will ever take your place in my life."

We sat that way for a while, and I thought that maybe I hadn't been behaving very maturely. My father had expected more of me. Even when I knew Fern had problems I had kept on being jealous, not realizing that my father was trying to help her. "I've been thinking," I said, breaking the silence. "Maybe I shouldn't come up for a while. Maybe it would be better if I stayed away."

My father shook his head. "Don't say that. I do think Fern needs a father, needs a lot of attention. If you can understand that and handle it, I don't want you to change your schedule."

"But that's the point. You said it—Fern needs a father and I think you can do it better if I'm not here. It gets mixed up when I'm around."

"You're a very perceptive and generous girl." My father sat back and looked at me. "Do you really want to do that?"

I nodded my head yes.

"But don't write me off," he said. "If you want to skip a few weekends I guess it wouldn't hurt, and it would give me a chance to spend time with Fern. Are you sure you want to do it?"

"Yes, I do." I hugged him and I knew I loved him a lot, but it would be a kind of a relief not to have to come for a while. I'd miss him, but I wouldn't miss the strain of Fern and her mother. Later, it might be better. Then I thought of Gerry. I wouldn't get to see him, either. That made me sit up.

"Remember Gerry, the boy who came over a couple weeks ago? He's on your soccer team. Is there any way I can call him? I'd like to see him over the weekend. I want to say good-bye to him."

"You mean Gerry Laine," my father said. "He's in the dorm, Tyler House. You can call and ask him over. How do you know him?"

"We met around here someplace."

"You don't have to say good-bye. You'll be coming back in a few weeks, won't you?"

"Yeah, sure," I said, but I wasn't so sure it would be so soon.

It wasn't until the next day, Saturday, that I caught up with Gerry after lunch. I went over to his dorm and found him on his way to the pond to go ice skating. He was alone and invited me to go with him. I didn't have any skates here—but Gerry said we could go over to the girls' dorm and borrow a pair. He seemed glad to see me and anxious to hang on to me.

We walked behind the tennis courts to the girls' dorm. It

was one of the newer red brick buildings. The outside was handsome, but the reception room we entered was pretty dreary. Not much furniture, and what there was looked rather shabby. A few girls were lounging around, and Gerry introduced me. One girl, Pam, said she had skates when he asked. The girls gave me the eye while Pam went for the skates, especially after Gerry told them who my father was. I didn't know whether I was getting Dad points or not.

The pond was a short distance from the school, and it was nice walking alongside Gerry, swinging our skates in the bright, cold sunshine. I felt comfortable with him, not worrying because we weren't talking much, or that he'd think me dumb and dull. He'd turn around and look at me every once in a while in a reassuring way, as if he was glad I was with him.

When we got there, not a soul was on the pond. It was great being all by ourselves in this one, cleared space in a woods. We couldn't even see the road when we were skating, only occasionally hear a car go by. We skated together, holding hands, and naturally falling into the same rhythm. I felt all the turmoil and strain of the past day and night dropping away.

We must have been skating for at least two hours when Gerry said he was hungry, and I realized that I was, too. We walked down the hill to the pizza parlor in the village. It was the middle of the afternoon so that, too, was pretty deserted; there was only one older couple sitting in a booth. We got into another booth and ordered a pizza for the two of us and tea to warm us up.

Then we began to talk. Gerry asked me why I hadn't come up the weekend before, so I told him about Fern's visit. He asked questions, not to pry, but because he was a friend, and before I knew it I was spilling out the whole story about Fern—her taking off and me following her, the whole bit. I swore him to secrecy because I certainly didn't want the story to get around the school. He promised and I felt sure he would keep his word.

"Fern's okay," Gerry said. "Paul said she was a weirdo, but he can be pretty nuts himself."

"Can he? I thought he was nice," I said.

Gerry gave me a funny smile. "He thinks the same about you. He asked me if I was seeing you. I think he would have liked to ask you out but he was worried Fern would do something stupid. She has a crush on him."

"I thought he had one on her, too. He seems to like her a lot." Even though I asked this question, my heart didn't miss a beat thinking about Paul. I'd almost forgotten I had ever thought I was crazy about him. That was in another time and had only been for a little while, anyway.

"I don't think he does," Gerry said. "But Paul doesn't stay with any girl very long. He moves around."

"Do you do that, too?"

Gerry looked deep into my eyes. "No. If I like a girl and she likes me, that's it. I don't need anybody else."

We kept looking at each other until our pizza arrived and we dug in. After I'd finished my first slice, I said, "Have you dated a lot of girls?"

Gerry finished chewing, then replied, "No, not a lot. I went around with a girl last summer—she was older than I was. We said we'd write to each other, but I think I wrote one letter and so did she, and that was the end of it. She was all right, but not as pretty as you."

"Are you going around with me?" The question sounded silly but I wanted to know.

Gerry laughed. "Round and round. Yeah, if you'll agree."

"But I won't be here for a while. I guess you'll find somebody else in school."

"Can't I come to see you? I'm allowed some weekends off. If you come here every weekend, it can't be far."

I hadn't thought of his coming to my mother's house. The thought made me very excited. "Sure, that would be terrific. It's easy; there's a bus that comes almost to our door."

"Great. I'll come next weekend. Is that okay?" He wasn't wasting any time. I was sure my mother wouldn't mind, so I told him it was.

When I came back to the house, Fern was in the garage with my father. They were rewiring an old lamp of my father's that hadn't been working for years. "She's a whiz," my father said. "Who'd have thought she was an electrician."

"I'm pretty good as a carpenter, too," Fern said, flushed with pleasure. "My father taught me a lot."

This Fern came as a surprise to me, and it was definitely out of character for the girl I had known. I felt a pang of jealousy watching the two of them working together, engrossed in what they were doing. But I still had the glow from my afternoon with Gerry, and I told myself that Fern needed my father more at this time than I did. Dad had told me not to write him off and I wasn't going to. It was more, I felt, as if I was lending him out for a time.

That evening the four of us played some board games, and it was almost as if we were a family. Not quite, but at least we were trying.

That night before we went up to bed I wondered if Fern was going to say anything to me. She didn't, which was a relief, but she did kiss me good night and give me what for her was an affectionate hug. I don't need you to say thank you, I thought, but I hope you appreciate having my father to yourself for a while.

When I left on Sunday, no one made a fuss, but my father did walk me down to the bus. "You're a terrific girl," he said to me, "or should I say young woman. I understand what you're doing and I appreciate it. I feel sure that when Fern is older she, too, will understand and be very grateful. I'll call you during the week; I don't want to be out of touch." Then he added something he hadn't said in a long time. "Remember me to your mother. Tell her she can be proud of you."

Riding home on the bus I felt a little sad but relieved also. While I knew I had to put my father aside for now, he'd be there when things got straightened out for Fern. In the meantime, Gerry would be in my life, I had my mother to count on, and I didn't mind getting rid of the knots in my stomach every weekend. I was better off than a lot of other kids. I'd be okay. When I got off at my stop I ran all the way home, where I knew my mother would be waiting for me.

About the Author

Born and raised in New York City, Hila Colman attended
Radcliffe College. Her stories and articles have appeared
in many periodicals, and some have been dramatized for
television. She is the author of a number of very popular
young adult novels, including NOT FOR LOVE and
NOBODY TOLD ME WHAT I NEED TO KNOW.

PATRICIA AKS

~~~~~~ SPEAKS TO ~~~~~~

YOUNG ADULTS

28